THE RUPA BOOK OF
SCHOOL QUIZ

G. Basu (b. 1943) is also the author of *General Quiz*. Born in a landowning family in former East Bengal, his interests span a wide range from liberal arts and social sciences to applied sciences like technology and medicine. Keenly interested in sports, he is a fanatical supporter of the East Bengal Club.

THE RUPA BOOK OF SCHOOL QUIZ

G. BASU

RUPA

Published by
Rupa Publications India Pvt. Ltd 2004
7/16, Ansari Road, Daryaganj
New Delhi 110002

Sales centres:

Allahabad Bengaluru Chennai
Hyderabad Jaipur Kathmandu
Kolkata Mumbai

ISBN: 978-81-716-7039-0

Seventeenth impression 2019

20 19 18 17

The moral right of the author has been asserted.

To
Ashima, with much love

CONTENTS

1

MONEY AND COMMERCE

1. What is disinflation, as distinguished from deflation?
2. What are the symptoms of stagflation?
3. What, in the USA, is a scam?
4. Which among the top ten exporters of oil in the world is not a member of the OPEC?
5. On which date did the Wall Street Crash begin?
6. What kind of arm-twisting is greenmail?
7. What is the legal definition of an infant?
8. What is hype, increasingly resorted to by corporate bodies?
9. Footsie in the financial world is not at all a naughty game; what is it?
10. What is a bear raid?
11. Bumf or bumph is the name of dull and boring papers and memoranda which executives dread dealing with. How was the word derived?
12. What has ergonomics to do with manufacture?
13. Why is OPEC called a cartel?
14. What is ALGOL?
15. What is dirty money?
16. In what way is cybernetics an important business science?

1
ANSWERS

1. Price rise slowing down, not as a result of a fall in the economic activity, but as a result of demand recession
2. Economic stagnation (high unemployment, slow or negative growth, etc.) accompanied by inflation
3. Business fraud
4. USSR (Top producer; second largest exporter)
5. 2 October 1929
6. Buying a large number of shares of a company and threatening to take it over, then selling back the shares to the company at a considerable profit
7. One under 18 years of age
8. Grossly exaggerated claims for a product, service, or a company, made through advertising
9. Financial Times Stock Exchange 100 Index (FT-SE 100)
10. Dumping a large number of a company's shares on the stock market to bring down their price
11. Shortened from bumfodder
12. It tries to obtain better efficiency from both men and machines through improvement in machine design, work routines, and the working environment
13. Because it controls the price, production, and marketing of its members' produce
14. Algorithmic language, a computer programming language
15. It is the extra remuneration paid for handling difficult or objectionable cargo or for working under physically disagreeable conditions
16. It produces theories relating to the control of complex human organizations and machine systems

17. In what relationship do the Benelux countries stand to the European Economic Community?
18. What does BASIC stand for?
19. What is a backhander in business deals?
20. What is a blocked currency?
21. What is a FERA company?
22. What is backward integration?
23. What does MRTPC stand for?
24. In computer parlance what is liveware?
25. What does a concert party do?
26. What is demand-pull inflation?
27. What is tax avoidance?
28. What is a pie chart?
29. When the discount is 25% + 10%, what is it effectively?
30. What are the yellow pages?
31. What is the importance of the Treaty of Rome?
32. What are collectibles?
33. Where is the New York Stock Exchange located?
34. At an annual rate of 10% inflation what will be the value of the rupee in ten years (Base year 1990)

17. They were the founder-members of the EEC
18. Beginner's All-purpose Symbolic Instruction Code, a simple computer-programming language
19. A bribe
20. A currency which you cannot take out of the country (the rouble, for example)
21. Foreign Exchange Regulation Act Company, one in which more than 40% of the shares are held by a foreign company or foreigners (e.g. ICI)
22. Acquiring companies which produce the raw materials a company uses
23. Monopolies and Restrictive Trade Practices Commission
24. Specialist staff who operate the hardware
25. Several companies acting together plan to take over another company
26. Price rise caused by the excess of demand over supply
27. Taking advantage of tax-saving provisions of the tax laws, e.g. by investing in government instruments, tax-free bonds, etc.
28. A circle is drawn and quantitative data are given as different-sized slices of the pie
29. 32.5%
30. A classified business telephone directory
31 Signed in March 1957 by Belgium, Netherlands, Luxembourg, France, West Germany, and Italy it created the EEC and the European Atomic Energy Community
32. Rare objects or objects likely to become rare which people buy, hoping that their price will rise, e.g. paintings, postage stamps, coins, autographs, etc.
33. 11 Wall Street, New York
34. 38.6p (In 25 years it will be 9.2p)

35. What does IBRD stand for?
36. What is the free lunch theorem?
37. What is meant when it is said that the bottom line of a company is healthy?
38. What is a leveraged company?
39. In advertising what is knocking copy?
40. What is a blue chip?
41. Why is such a share called a blue chip?
42. Why were Krugerrands much fancied before many governments banned their sale?
43. Why is the term synergy often used in the merger of two companies?
44. Who is a rentier?
45. How does the Peter Principle relate to the corporate and public sector ladders?
46. What exactly does Parkinson's Law postulate?
47. What does MICR stand for in bank cheques?
48. 'Madison Avenue thinks ...' Why should its thinking be any more important than, say, Second Avenue's?
49. What is an inherent vice in a product?
50. What does a white knight do, not in Alice's wonderland, but in the corporate jungle?

2

WORLD AFFAIRS

51. Who was the most prominent member of the Gang of Four who were held responsible for the excesses of the Cultural Revolution and accused of trying to seize power after the deaths of Mao Tse-Tung and Chou En-Lai?
52. Which were the years of the Cultural Revolution in China?

35. International Bank for Reconstruction and Development, i.e. the World Bank
36. That there is no such thing as a free lunch
37. It has made a profit
38. A company with a high degree of long-term debt in relation to its equity (i.e. share capital)
39. An advertisement which directly attacks a rival's product
40. Share of a reputed well-established company with a steady growth
41. In casino gambling the chips of the highest value are blue in colour
42. South African coins, they contained one ounce of pure gold
43. Synergy is two things working together producing an effect greater than the sum of their individual effects. Also known as $2 + 2 = 5$
44. One whose income is derived from any source of capital — interest on securities, dividends, rent from property, etc.
45. It states that employees and directors are promoted until they attain their level of inefficiency
46. Work expands to fill the time available for its completion
47. Magnetic Ink Character Recognition
48. It is the centre of the U.S. advertisement industry
49. The tendency to deteriorate, e.g. fruit will rot
50. A company that comes to the rescue of another which is threatened with a takeover bid

2
ANSWERS

51. Jiang Quing, Mao's widow
52. 1966-69

53. The Long March: what, when, from where to where?
54. Why is Mr. Gorbachev's Glasnost regarded as a breath of fresh air in the Soviet society?
55. What is Mr. Gorbachev's Perestroika?
56. Who instituted the National Health Service, which provides free medical treatment and hospitalization to British citizens?
57. Which territory of Hong Kong was leased by the Chinese to the British for 99 years?
58. When is the 99-year lease of the New Territories in Hong Kong due to expire?
59. What did the Camp David Accord (1979) seek to achieve?
60. When was Bangladesh born as a nation?
61. When was East Bengal renamed East Pakistan by the rulers of Pakistan?
62. Pakistan has had fourteen rulers (including Mr. Jatoi) since its birth. Whose tenure has been the shortest?
63. Which Pakistani ruler so far has had the longest innings?
64. Was Yugoslavia a member of the Soviet bloc, known as the Comintern?
65. What was Marshal Tito's claim to the undisputed leadership of Yugoslavians from 1945 to 1980?
66. Which Communist leader was the first to break with Soviet Russia to pursue an independent national Communism?
67. Who did the Soviets install in Hungary as Premier after crushing the revolution led by Imre Nagy?
68. Who are the major exporters of arms in the world?
69. When did Soviet Russia invade Czechoslovakia to put an end to the liberalization that was taking place in the country?

53. The 6000-mile march undertaken by the Red Army under the leadership of Mao Tse-Tung; in 1934-35; escaping from Nationalist forces in Jiangxi province westward to Shaanxi province
54. Glasnost is freedom of expression, in speech as well as writing
55. Economic restructuring; gradual loosening of State control
56. Aneurin Bevan, Minister of Health in the Labour government
57. The New Territories
58. 1997
59. Peace between Israel and Egypt
60. 26 March 1971
61. 1955
62. General Iskander Mirza (less than a month, October 1958)
63. President Zia-ul-Haq, 11 years 1 month, July 1977-August 1988. He beats Ayub Khan by five months
64. Yes, but Tito left the Comintern in 1948
65. His leadership of the partisan movement against the German occupation and his independent liberal policies
66. Marshal Josip Broz Tito of Yugoslavia (1948)
67. Janos Kadar
68. The USSR
69. August 1968 (Dubcek was removed from office in 1969)

70. Alexander Dubcek became the Communist Party Secretary in Czechoslovakia in 1968. What was his secretaryship distinguished for?

71. What was the independent (as distinguished from Communist-controlled) trade union federation which was formed in Poland in 1980 called?

72. Why was President Anwar al-Sadat assassinated in 1981?

73. In which year did Sikkim become the 22nd State of India?

74. Since its inception Israel has been subject to four fierce attacks from its neighbouring States, although each time the attackers lost. When did Israel carry war to a neighbouring State?

75. When were the two Germanys unified after World War II?

76. Which country was divided to carve out the territory of Israel?

77. When was the Organization of Petroleum Exporting Countries (OPEC) founded?

78. When the OPEC was founded in 1960 it had thirteen members. How many does it have now?

79. When did the full-scale border war start between Iraq and Iran over navigation rights in the Shatt-al-Arab waterway?

80. When the Iranian militants seized the U.S. embassy in Teheran and held its occupants hostage, what were their demands?

81. When did Ayatollah Ruhollah Khomeini assume power in Iran?

82. How did the rule of Salvador Allende Gossens, the Marxist President of Chile, end?

83. Why are the Sandinistas so called?

84. Who overthrew the Somozan regime in Nicaragua?

85. What was the Bay of Pigs fiasco?

70. Liberal policies and gradual democratization
71. Solidarity
72. Muslim fundamentalists didn't like his making a peace treaty with Israel in the Camp David Accord, and bumped him off
73. 1975
74. In 1982, against Lebanon, from whose bases the PLO was conducting intermittent raids into Israeli territory
75. 3 October 1990
76. Palestine
77. 1960
78. Twenty-one
79. September 1980
80. That the Shah of Iran, who had taken refuge in the USA, should be returned to Iran
81. 1979
82. Overthrown in a bloody (Allende was killed) military coup led by General Augusto Pinochet in 1973
83. They are named after an early guerrilla hero, Augusto Cesar Sandino
84. The Sandinistas (Sandinist National Liberation Front)
85. Unsuccessful US-supported attempt by anti-Castro exiles to invade Cuba at the bay. Most were killed; those taken prisoner were ransomed for $53 million

86. Who did Fidel Castro supplant in Cuba by his long guerrilla warfare?
87. Where are the headquarters of the North Atlantic Treaty Organization?
88. In which spy novel, published in 1963, does the Berlin Wall play a crucial part?
89. How long was the Berlin Wall?
90. How long did the Berlin Wall divide East and West Germany?
91. Two countries withdrew from the Warsaw Treaty Organization because of Moscow's suppression of democratic movements. Which countries?
92. What is the Communist bloc's equivalent of North Atlantic Treaty Organization?
93. What is the 38th Parallel?
94. How long did the United States actively fight in Vietnam to aid the South Vietnam regime?
95. Who were the participants in the Six Day War in 1967?
96. When did the Korean War take place?
97. What happened at Dien Bien Phu?
98. Which English king abdicated the throne to marry the woman of his choice?
99. Which countries in the world are known to have made their own atomic bombs?
100. When did the Iraqi armed invasion of Kuwait occur?

3

1914-45 : EUROPE'S LONG DARK NIGHT

101. How long did World War I last?
102. Who were the Central Powers in World War I?
103. What was the treaty which ended World War I called?

86. Fulgencio Batista
87. Brussels, Belgium
88. John Le Carré's *The Spy Who Came in from the Cold*
89. 47 km
90. 13 August 1961 - 9 November 1989
91. Czechoslovakia and Albania
92. Warsaw Treaty Organization
93. The line dividing North Korea from South Korea
94. 1961-73
95. Israel versus Egypt, Syria, and Jordan
96. 1950-53 (Between North Koreans aided by Chinese 'volunteers' and the South Koreans aided by the U.N. contingents)
97. The French were defeated by the Viet Minh: withdrew from Vietnam (1952)
98. King Edward VIII (1936)
99. USA, USSR, Britain, France, China, and India
100. 2 August 1990

3
ANSWERS

101. August 1914 - November 1918
102. Germany, Austria-Hungary, and Turkey
103. Treaty of Versailles

104. Which statesman considered World War I necessary 'to make the world safe for democracy'?
105. Who were the Axis Powers in World War II?
106. In which year did Benito Mussolini attack and conquer Abyssinia?
107. Before World War II Britain and France entered into a pact with Hitler, trying to appease him by ceding much of Czechoslovakian territory to Germany. What is the name of the pact?
108. When did Russia and Germany, ideological enemies, conclude a non-aggression pact which caused great dissension among the Communists all over the world?
109. What was Anschluss?
110. When did Hitler invade Poland to start World War II?
111. What was Operation Barbarossa which Hitler launched in June 1941?
112. What was the Battle of Britain in World War II?
113. Why is Pearl Harbour a landmark in World War II?
114. What role did General Rommel play in World War II?
115. What was D Day in World War II?
116. Apart from Auschwitz, name two concentration camps run by the Nazis where organized killings of the Jews took place.
117. Which city in Germany was completely destroyed by R.A.F. bombing (786 bombers, 2647 tons of bombs dropped) followed by two more U.S. Air Force raids?
118. What is the meaning of Putsch?

104. President Woodrow Wilson of the USA
105. Germany, Italy, and Japan
106. 1936
107. Munich Pact, 1938
108. August 1939
109. Union of Austria and Germany by forcible occupation of Austria on 13 March 1938
110. 1 September 1939
111. Attack on Soviet Russia
112. The air battle fought over southern England between the RAF and the Luftwaffe (July-October 1940)
113. On 7 December 1941 the Japanese bombed the U.S. Pacific fleet moored in Pearl Harbour in Hawaii and brought in the USA to war
114. His Afrika Korps fought in North Africa successfully, and nearly took Cairo. (He was however defeated in the battle of El Alamein by General Montgomery's troops)
115. 6 June 1944, the date of Allied landing on the Normandy beach, heralding their unstoppable march to Berlin
116. Belzec, Sobibor, Treblinka, Majdanek, Theresienstadt, Birkenau, Chelmno (The other concentration camps often killed through neglect and starvation)
117. Dresden; 13-15 February 1945. (Read Kurt Vonnegut: *Slaughterhouse-5*)
118. German word, meaning forcible takeover of a government

119. Counting from the date of the invasion of Poland to V-J Day (Victory over Japan, the day of Japanese surrender) how long did World War II last?

120. Which countries in Europe remained neutral in World War II?

121. Apart from the unparalleled heroism of the RAF Fighter Command, what contributed to the British success against the Luftwaffe air raids on Britain?

122. What were the main British fighter aircraft in World War II?

123. Which was the most widely used fighter aircraft of the Germans in World War II?

124. What happened on the Night of the Long Knives in June 1934?

125. What role did Dr. Joseph Mengele play in Nazi Germany?

126. Does Zyklon-B mean anything to you in the context of Nazi Germany?

127. Before his suicide (30 April 1945) Hitler expelled from the Nazi Party two of its prominent members. Who were they?

128. When did Hitler, as the leader of the National Socialists, become Chancellor of Germany?

129. How long did Hitler say the Third Reich would last?

130. Hitler used to say that whoever wanted to understand National Socialist (Nazi) Germany must know a certain musician. Who?

131. What was Operation Valkyrie in Nazi Germany?

132. In World War II which Russian General repulsed the German attack on Moscow?

133. How did Mussolini meet his end?

134. What was Hideki Tojo's role in World War II?

135. What was Hitler's father's family name before he changed it to Hiedler?

119. Exactly six years
120. Ireland, Sweden, Switzerland, Spain, and Portugal
121. The Radar; the Germans hadn't developed it
122. Spitfires and Hurricanes
123. Messerschmitt
124. Hitler ordered the killing of his enemies of the Nazi Party (Ernst Roehm was killed a day later)
125. Doctor at the Auschwitz Concentration Camp who selected from the deportees who should be sent to the gas chambers. He also experimented with the living and the dead in his racial experiments
126. Crystallized prussic acid gas patented by IG Farben, used in the gas chambers to exterminate Jews and others
127. Goering and Himmler
128. 30 January 1933
129. 1000 years
130. Richard Wagner (1813-83)
131. The unsuccessful attempt to kill Hitler with a time bomb on 20 July 1944
132. General Georgi Zhukov
133. Caught with his mistress by Italian Partisans while trying to escape into Italy and executed on 28 April 1945. Their bodies were strung up on lamp-posts in Milan
134. Japanese General and Premier, in total control of the Japanese war machine. Tried as a war criminal and executed
135. Schicklgruber

136. How many Jews were exterminated in Nazi Germany in government-organized operations?
137. Which among the following criminals were not sentenced to death by the International Military Tribunal which sat at Nuremberg between November 1945 and September 1946: Alfred Jodl, Joachim von Ribbentrop, Rudolf Hess, Hans Frank, Walther Funk?
138. What was Albert Speer's position in Hitler's war machine?
139. Which were the two parties fighting the Spanish Civil War?
140. When did the Spanish Civil War start?
141. In World War II, what was Operation Sealion?
142. Who was Hitler's propaganda minister?
143. What ultimately happened to Dr. Goebbels?
144. What was Hermann Goering's role in World War II?
145. What was Gestapo, the secret Nazi police, an acronym for?
146. Who was the Supreme Commander of the Allied Expeditionary Force which directed the Allied offensive in Europe?
147. What happened to Adolf Eichmann, who planned and oversaw the mass murders of millions of Jews, after World War II?
148. Which was the date of Germany's surrender in World War II?
149. When was the atomic bomb dropped on Hiroshima?
150. Who ordered the dropping of the atomic bomb on Japan in World War II?

136. Nearly six million, although the actual number may have been larger
137. Hess and Funk
138. Minister for Armaments
139. The Republicans (Communists) and the Nationalists (Fascists)
140. July 1936
141. Codename of Hitler's plan to invade Britain by crossing the English Channel
142. Dr. Goebbels (Joseph Paul)
143. The day following Hitler's suicide he poisoned his wife and children and shot himself
144. He was the chief of Luftwaffe, the German air force
145. GEheimes STAatsPOlizei
146. General Dwight David Eisenhower
147. Kidnapped by Jewish agents from Argentina, tried by the Israelis, and hanged in 1962
148. 7 May 1945
149. 6 August 1945
150. President Truman (He didn't consult his Service Chiefs)

4

HISTORY

151. Where was the Battle of Waterloo fought in which Napoleon was finally defeated?

152. Which Russian emperor was forced to abdicate as a result of the Russian Revolution of 1917?

153. Who was the last of the Aztec kings with whose murder the civilization of the Aztecs came to an end?

154. During which ancient Roman emperor's reign did Rome attain the height of cultural eminence, nurturing such talents as Vergil, Ovid, Livy, and Horace?

155. During whose reign did ancient Greece excel in a cultural development rarely equalled in world history?

156. Who brought an end to the Holy Roman Empire, which was much less than an empire, and not all that holy either?

157. Who was the founder of the ancient Persian empire?

158. When did the great civilization of Egypt, which began in 3110 B.C., end?

159. When did the Babylonian civilization flourish in Mesopotamia?

160. When did the All-India Congress Committee give the call for the Quit India movement?

161. What was 26 January, now observed as Republic Day, originally observed as?

162. Which Sikh ruler foresaw the complete domination of India by the British and referring to the map of India said, *'sab lal ho jayega'*?

163. Who was the Governor-General of India when Tipu Sultan was finally defeated by the British?

4
ANSWERS

151. Near Brussels, Belgium
152. Czar Nicholas II
153. Montezuma (murdered by Cortes after defeat)
154. Emperor Augustus (63 B.C. - A.D. 14)
155. Pericles, *c.* 495-429 B.C.
156. Napoleon I. 1806
157. Cyrus the Great, mid-6th century B.C.
158. With the conquest by Alexander, 332 B.C.
159. *c.* 1750 B.C. - 538 B.C.
160. 8 August 1942
161. Independence Day, 1930
162. Maharaja Ranjit Singh
163. Lord Wellesley

164. On the walls of which building of the Mughal period is to be found the following inscription?
    If on Earth there is an Eden of bliss,
    It is this, it is this, none but this.
165. Whose army did the British defeat in the Battle of Plassey (1757) to mark the beginning of the British empire in India?
166. With whose death did the Mughal empire become extinct?
167. Which action of a Mughal emperor turned the Sikhs into implacable enemies of the Mughals?
168. Which battle really marked the real beginning of the Mughal empire in India?
169. How old was Akbar when he was proclaimed king?
170. Which Afghan king of India is credited with the introduction of a brilliant administrative system?
171. Who was the descendant of Timur and Chingiz Khan who laid the foundation of an empire in India?
172. Which king built the Sun Temple at Konarak?
173. About which Muslim emperor can these questions be asked: Was he a genius or a lunatic? An idealist or a visionary? A bloodthirsty tyrant or a benevolent king? A heretic or a devout Mussalman?
174. With whose death did the Tughlaq dynasty come to an end?
175. 'He shed more innocent blood than even Pharaoh was guilty of' — about which Muslim emperor was this written?
176. In whose reign did Fa Hien, the Chinese traveller, visit India?
177. Which king crushed the Huns who ruled over a considerable part of India till around the first quarter of sixth century A.D.?

164. Diwan-i-Khas
165. Nawab Siraj-ud-daulah
166. Bahadur Shah II (1862)
167. Emperor Jahangir's execution of the fifth Sikh Guru, Arjan (1606)
168. The second battle of Panipat (1557)
169. Thirteen
170. Sher Shah Suri
171. Babur
172. Narasimha I (1238-1264)
173. Muhammad bin Tughlaq
174. Sultan Mahmud (A.D. 1413)
175. Ala-ud-din Khalji
176. Chandragupta II
177. Yashodharman

178. In whose reign did Asvaghosa, philosopher, poet, and dramatist, compose *Buddhacharita*?
179. Who was the Kushana emperor who laid the foundation of an Indian empire by becoming complete master of the Indian borderland?
180. Can you give the dates of Asoka's reign?
181. One of Buddha's close relatives was a relentless enemy of his, once having arranged to have let loose on Buddha's path a mad elephant. Who was he?
182. In books of ancient history the word millennium is frequently used. What period of time does it indicate?
183. What does Mohenjo-Daro mean?
184. Where did Harsha rule?
185. What is the latest date assigned to the earliest ruins of Mohenjo-Daro and Harappa?
186. Whose victory over the Rajput chief, Prithviraj, laid the foundation of Muslim dominion of northern India?
187. Qutb-ud-din was the founder of the Slave dynasty. Whose slave was he?
188. Where were the French defeated in the French Indo-China war?
189. When were the great pyramids of Egypt built?
190. Who founded the Republic of Indonesia and became its first President?
191. When was Pakistan defeated in the Bangladesh War?
192. Before the Meiji Restoration who ruled Japan?
193. Why were the Communists forced to undertake the Long March (1934-35)?
194. Who was the first President of the Turkish Republic after the abolition of the Sultanate?
195. When were North and South Vietnam unified by the Communists?

178. Kanishka
179. Kadphises I
180. *c.* 269 B.C. - *c.* 232 B.C.
181. Devadatta
182. 1000 years
183. Mound of the Dead
184. Kanauj
185. 2700 B.C.
186. Muhammad of Ghur (A.D. 1192)
187. Muhammad of Ghur
188. Dienbienphu (1954)
189. Between 2680 B.C. and 2565 B.C.
190. Sukarno
191. December 1971
192. The Tokugawa Shogunate
193. Chiang Kai-Shek had started purging his former Communist allies in the Chinese civil war
194. Kemal Ataturk (1923-38)
195. 1976

196. Why did the Conservatives, the Church, the army, and the Fascists join together to oppose the Republicans in the Spanish Civil War?
197. When did Mussolini seize power in Italy to make it a Fascist State?
198. When was the State of Israel proclaimed?
199. Whose assassination at Sarajevo on 28 June 1914 led to World War I?
200. When was monarchy abolished in France?

5

OUR GALAXY

201. How long does light take to travel from the sun to the earth?
202. What is the speed of light?
203. What is a parsec?
204. How far is the nearest star to earth, Proxima Centauri?
205. How far away is Sirius, a star 28 times brighter than the sun, from the earth?
206. Galaxies have three kinds of shape: spiral, elliptical, or irregular. What is the shape of our galaxy?
207. What is the distance between the earth and the Andromeda galaxy, which can only be seen as a distant smear in the horizon on winter evenings from the northern hemisphere?
208. Sir James Jeans speculated on the death of the sun. For how many more years is the sun still good?
209. What is the sun's size compared with the solar system?
210. At what speed does the sun rotate on its axis?
211. What is the distance of the sun from the earth in km?
212. What is the inner core temperature of the sun?

196. The Republicans were a leftist coalition
197. October 1922
198. 14 May 1948
199. Archduke Francis Ferdinand (heir-apparent to the Austro-Hungarian throne)
200. September 1792

5
ANSWERS

201. 8 minutes
202. 300,000 km per second
203. A distance of 3.26 light years
204. 4.22 light years
205. 8.7 light years
206. Spiral
207. 2,120,000 light years
208. 10,000 million years
209. 99.866% of all matter
210. 7050 km per hour
211. 150 million km
212. 16 million °K

213. How hot is the corona of the sun, which is a thin gas extending to about 15 million km from the surface of the sun and which is clearly visible during a total eclipse of the sun?

214. What are sunspots?

215. Which is the planet closest to the sun and what is the distance?

216. What is the area of the largest sunspot so far observed?

217. How long exactly does the earth take to orbit the sun?

218. Which is the largest planet in our galaxy?

219. How long does Pluto take to orbit the sun?

220. There is a considerable difference in Mercury's temperature between the sides facing the sun and the dark side. What are the temperatures?

221. Which gas does Venus's atmosphere mostly consist of?

222. Are the two poles of the earth equal in radius?

223. What is the total surface area of the earth?

224. What is the average height of the earth above the sea level?

225. How much time passes between two new moons?

226. What is the mean distance of the moon from the earth at nearest point?

227. How many moons does Jupiter have?

228. What are the bright rings around Saturn?

229. The five satellites of Uranus are named after four characters in Shakespeare and one in Pope. Name them.

230. Which new planet was spotted in 1930?

231. Which is the largest constellation of stars in the sky?

232. Which stars are hotter — those which give out a bluish-white light or those which emit a yellow light?

233. What kind of a star is a red giant?

234. What kind of a star is a white dwarf?

213. 1 million °C
214. Areas on the surface of the sun where the temperature is lower, about 4000°C, and the surface therefore looks dark
215. Mercury; 58 million km
216. 18 million sq km
217. 365.25 days
218. Jupiter; more than eleven times larger than the earth and 318 times heavier
219. 248 years and 142 days
220. 400°C and −150°C
221. Carbon dioxide, 95%
222. No, the south is 45 metres shorter than the north
223. 510 million sq km
224. 857 m
225. 29 days, 7 hours, 44 minutes
226. 376,284 km
227. 16
228. These are composed of millions of small pieces of ice-coated rocks
229. Ariel, Miranda, Oberon, Titania, and Umbriel
230. Pluto
231. Hydra
232. The former; temperatures up to 100,000°C
233. A star that is coming to the end of its life
234. It is a red giant that has used up all its fuel and is dead

235. What is a black hole?
236. What is a supernova?
237. What are asteroids?
238. The northern polar lights are called *Aurorae Borealis*; what are the southern polar lights called?
239. At what interval does Haley's Comet appear?
240. How much meteoric dust falls on the earth's surface in a year?
241. When was the first artificial satellite, Sputnik, put in space?
242. Which space satellite crashed onto the moon in 1959?
243. Which country put the first man into space in 1961?
244. On which date did Neil Armstrong and Edwin Aldren land on the moon?
245. Which gas dominates the earth's atmosphere?
246. Which atmospheric layer lies immediately above the earth's surface, up to a height of 10 km?
247. What is the charge of electricity in lightning?
248. Which is the largest natural satellite in space?
249. Who wrote *Dialogue Concerning the Two Chief World Systems*?
250. What are quasars or quasi-stellar objects?

6

LIVING CREATURES

251. Which bird is the most deadly enemy of snakes?
252. About the ways of which animal do naturalists know the least?
253. Which bird holds the record for long-distance migratory flying?
254. Which animal can cut down a tree with its teeth?
255. Which living creature has the longest average life span?

235. It is created when an immense star has collapsed, leaving a rim only a few kilometres in diameter
236. A dying star, at least five times the weight of the sun; when it collapses it becomes up to 100,000,000 times brighter as it erupts in a tremendous nuclear explosion
237. Bits of debris left after the formation of the solar system, or the remains of a disintegrated planet
238. *Aurorae Australis*
239. 76 years
240. Up to 5 million tonnes
241. 4 October 1957
242. The Soviet satellite Luna II
243. USSR; Yuri Gagarin in Vostok I
244. 20 July 1969
245. Nitrogen; 78.09%
246. Troposphere
247. 10,000 amps
248. Ganymede, Jupiter's satellite. It is larger than the planet Mercury
249. Galileo Galilei (1564-1642). Upheld the Copernican system and marked a turning point in scientific and philosophical thought
250. Starlike celestial objects, most luminous and most distant in the universe, which are receding from our galaxy with speeds as great as 80% of the speed of light.

6
ANSWERS

251. Secretary bird
252. Gorillas
253. The Arctic tern
254. Beaver
255. Tortoise

256. Animals living closely together often mate with their close relatives. Which animal rarely does so?
257. What is conditioned reflex?
258. Who discovered conditioned reflex?
259. What is the study of animals in their natural habitat called?
260. How many species of birds are there in the world?
261. Which animal, man included, has the longest gestation period?
262. Which countries are vampire birds native of?
263. Which is the fastest bird in the world?
264. Which is the most dangerous river fish to man?
265. Which is the largest fish in the world?
266. Who has the largest eyes in the animal kingdom?
267. What are the main characteristics of arachnida?
268. How many named species of insects are there in all?
269. In which geological period did the first bird, Acheopterix, appear?
270. Who introduced the scientific classification of plants and animals by their genus and species names?
271. In honeybees what do fertilized and unfertilized eggs produce?
272. The Centaur Greek mythology is half man and half beast. Which beast?
273. What is the main difference between a frog and a toad?
274. How does a squid move in water?
275. How does the crab manage to see all round?
276. Where does the Bird of Paradise, perhaps the most beautiful in the world, live?
277. What is peculiar about the duckbilled platypus?
278. Which country has the largest population of domestic cats?

256. Prairie dogs
257. Behaviour of an organism which becomes dependent on an event preceding it, e.g. giving a dog food after ringing a bell. Soon, at the ringing of the bell the dog will salivate.
258. I.P. Pavlov
259. Ethology
260. Nearly 9000
261. African elephant, 640 days
262. Mexico; Paraguay
263. The white-throated spine-tailed swift; speed 170 km/h
264. Piranha, especially in the Amazon
265. Rhincodon typus or the whale shark, up to 43 tonnes
266. The giant squid
267. Four pairs of legs and two parts of the body
268. Around 850,000
269. Jurassic, 195 million years ago
270. Carolus Linnaeus (1707-78), Swedish naturalist
271. Unfertilized eggs: male drones; fertilized eggs: female workers and queens
272. Horse
273. Toad: dry, warty skin; frog: smooth, moist skin
274. By the principle of jet propulsion; it squirts out water from its body with great force
275. Its eyes are set on a stalk that can move 360°
276. Australia and New Guinea
277. It lays eggs, but when these are hatched it suckles the young
278. The United States of America

279. What is special about the saliva of a mosquito?
280. Why can't koala bears be bred in zoos?
281. What is biological control of crops and plants?
282. What is a living fossil?
283. Which bird is featured on the Great Seal of the USA?
284. What is parthenogenesis?
285. Which Tiger Reserve in India is your best bet for viewing tigers?
286. The Rann of Kutch has an animal found nowhere else in the world. Which is it?
287. Which is the largest of the tiger species?
288. Who mates with whom to produce a mule?
289. In which country did the recently extinct bird dodo live?
290. In the study of plants and animals the old world and the new world are often mentioned. Which is the new world?
291. Which country supplied all the world's zoos with the white tiger?
292. Which animal is the teddy bear?
293. The armoured dinosaur of northern Europe could weigh up to 1.75 tonnes. How much did its brain weigh?
294. How many rabbits can be produced from a pair of them in three years?
295. Where is the black swan to be found in abundance?
296. Which bird's eggs are the largest?
297. Which creature's mode of choosing a mate is depositing a pebble at her feet?
298. What is the study of the ancient forms of life called?
299. What is a cygnet?
300. What are the giant flying lizards, now extinct, called?

279. It contains a decoagulant
280. They eat the leaves of only four varieties of eucalyptus leaves which grow in Australia
281. Introducing pests' natural enemies to eradicate them
282. A creature which has remained unchanged for millions of years, e.g. dragonfly
283. The Bald Eagle
284. Reproduction in which an unfertilized egg develops into a new individual
285. Kanha National Park (M.P.)
286. The Asiatic Wild Ass
287. The Siberian Tiger
288. A male ass with a mare
289. Mauritius
290. North and South Americas
291. India (Rewa)
292. Koala
293. About 70 g. The human brain weighs between 1 and 1.5 kg
294. 13 million
295. Round the coasts of Australia
296. Ostrich
297. Penguin
298. Palaeontology
299. A young swan
300. Pterodactyls

7
PLANT KINGDOM

301. Purslane leaves are used as herbs in some cookery; by what name is the plant commonly known?
302. From which plant is mescaline, a powerful hallucinogenic, obtained?
303. Although tea plants can grow up to 30', at what maximum height are they pruned for commercial production?
304. What is hydroponics?
305. Which State in India is the least afforested?
306. Which Austrian monk experimenting on garden peas discovered the principles of genetics?
307. Which plant growing in high altitudes and regarded in Europe as a symbol of purity is protected in Switzerland by law?
308. How is the name of Lancelot Brown (1716-83), also known as Capability Brown, associated with trees?
309. What is India's share in the total afforested area of the world?
310. The fibres of which plant give us linen?
311. Apart from growing wild, in what important respect is wild rice different from rice as we know it?
312. In which season in America and Canada do deciduous trees shed their leaves?
313. Of which State in India is the greatest part covered with forests?
314. Which fruit is not really a fruit but a flower?
315. Which is the largest and most important family of conifers?
316. From which plant or tree is essence of vanilla obtained?

7
ANSWERS

301. Portulaca
302. From the Peyote cactus
303. 5′
304. Soilless agriculture
305. Haryana
306. Mendel, Gregor Johann (1822-84)
307. Edelweiss
308. He was a landscape gardener and created such places as the lake at Blenheim Palace and Chatworth Park
309. 2%
310. Flax
311. The tall aquatic plant belongs to the grass family. Originally eaten by the American Indians, it is now regarded as a delicacy
312. Fall
313. Arunachal Pradesh
314. Fig
315. Pine
316. A species of orchid

317. How long does it take for hardwood forests to be replaced?
318. Which country accounts for most of the world's supply of teak?
319. How long ago did leafy trees, coniferous, first appear on the earth?
320. How long ago did algae, the most primitive plant life in the world, develop?
321. Which is the latest State in India to start producing high grade tea?
322. From which tree does the solidified milky juice used in chewing gums come?
323. Quinine is obtained from the cinchona tree; what is strychnine obtained from?
324. Which country in the world first learnt the use of cotton?
325. How was the alkaloid which gives tobacco its narcotic and soothing effect named?
326. Which State in India grows cloves, cinnamon, and black pepper in profusion?
327. To which countries are we indebted for the most popular tuber, potato?
328. To which native tribe is the world indebted for sweetcorn or maize?
329. Where is the famous Valley of Flowers located?
330. Which country is the largest habitat of the sunflower?
331. Where do lichens, which grow on Arctic rocks, get their food from?
332. Where do giant cactuses, up to 15 m high, grow?
333. What really is the name of the fruit which goes by the name of orange in India?
334. Of which country is the maple leaf the national symbol?
335. Which is the tallest tree in the world, recorded to a height of 112 m?
336. What is a drupe?

317. More than a hundred years
318. Burma
319. 395,000,0υυ years ago
320. 2,000,000,000 years ago
321. Sikkim
322. Sapodilla
323. The *nux vomica* tree
324. India, 3000 B.C.
325. From Jean Nicot, French ambassador, who presented the seeds of the plant to Queen Catherine of Medici
326. Kerala
327. Chile and Peru
328. The American Indians
329. The Garhwal Himalayas
330. USSR, Ukraine
331. The air
332. Arizona desert
333. Tangerine
334. Canada
335. Californian Redwood (pine)
336. A fleshy fruit with an inner hard stone enclosing the seed; apricot, peach, etc.

337. How do conifers, cone-bearing evergreens, propagate their species?
338. Where is the Valley of the Roses located?
339. Although Holland is now the land of tulips, from which country was the flower originally introduced in Europe?
340. How old should a cork tree be before it can be stripped of its bark?
341. Of the wood of which tree are cricket bats made?
342. Which is the country of origin of the common Indian flower, marigold (*genda*)?
343. Where is the largest natural forest in the world?
344. Which is the most massive tree in the world?
345. Which is the world's oldest *living* tree, 4600 years old?
346. Which is the world's oldest flowering plant, 180 million years old?
347. Which tree was considered sacred by the Greeks?
348. What are the Spermatophyta division of plants?
349. Which was the country of origin of the dahlia?
350. Where is the largest manmade forest in the world?

8

THE SCIENCES

351. Who are the propounders of the theory of chemical evolution of life?
352. Where did Charles Darwin find conclusive evidence for his theory of evolution?
353. Name the first among earth satellites in the sky.
354. Which star doesn't change its position in the night sky?
355. What is solid carbon dioxide called?
356. Which metals are mixed to make an alloy?

337. Through cones, which are dropped on the ground
338. Bulgaria
339. Turkey
340. About sixteen years
341. Willow
342. Mexico
343. Northern USSR, 1,100,000,000 hectares
344. Giant Sequoia, in California, 6100 tonnes
345. Californian Bristlecone Pine
346. Maidenhair plant or the Japanese Ginko
347. Olive
348. Those which bear seeds
349. Mexico
350. New Zealand; Kaingora State Forest, 151,096 hectares

8
ANSWERS

351. J.B.S. Haldane and A.I. Oparin
352. Galapagos Islands
353. The moon
354. Polaris
355. Dry ice
356. Any two or more

357. What did C.S. Cockerell invent?
358. Which calculator has two log scales moving alongside each other?
359. In tropical climates why should white clothes be preferred?
360. What does a tachometer record?
361. What does the Beaufort scale measure?
362. 'The harbour is only four fathoms deep' — how deep in feet would that be?
363. Which letter of the alphabet measures the size of a computer's memory?
364. In computer parlance what is hard copy?
365. Fire and brimstone were mentioned as agents of destruction in the Bible. What is brimstone?
366. Which acid in diluted form makes vinegar?
367. What is added to rubber to make it heat and cold resistant?
368. Which chemical compound is likely to replace petrol?
369. How was Einstein's Theory of Relativity experimentally proved correct?
370. What is the filament of a light bulb made of?
371. Who piloted the first space flight?
372. Who is the inventor of the 'superbug' which fights oil spills in the sea?
373. Who invented the safety pin?
374. What is the mathematical formulation of Einstein's Theory of Relativity?
375. What is the absolute zero in temperature?
376. What is the name of the first computer language?
377. Who was the first scientist to use the zero as a mathematical number?
378. How many Roman numerals are there in all?
379. What is the Mohs' scale used for?
380. What are the boiling and freezing points of a Centigrade thermometer?

357. The hovercraft
358. Slide rule
359. White reflects the maximum heat; other colours partly or wholly absorb them
360. The number of engine revolutions per minute
361. The force of wind
362. 24 feet
363. K
364. A printout
365. Sulphur
366. Acetic acid
367. Carbon black
368. Ethanol
369. By a solar eclipse
370. Tungsten
371. John Young and Robert Crippen
372. Ananda M. Chakrabarty
373. Walter Hunt
374. $E = mc^2$; where E = energy, m = mass, and c = velocity of light
375. $-273°C$
376. PLANKALKUEL
377. Brahmagupta
378. Seven (M, D, C, L, X, V, I)
379. To indicate the hardness of minerals, e.g. quartz
380. 100° and 0°

381. Which prefix would you use to indicate a million SI Units of something, e.g. watt?
382. What does the MKS system of units stand for?
383. What are nerve gases mostly derived from?
384. What is the scientific name of laughing gas?
385. Which element has the highest atomic number, 103?
386. Which chemical element has the atomic number 1?
387. Which vegetable, used in salads, contains Vitamin E?
388. What is 'radar' the abbreviation of?
389. What did Charles Babbage call his first computer?
390. Why aren't electric motor cars still viable?
391. From which mineral is aluminium extracted?
392. If you were a mycologist what would you study?
393. Among metals which is the lightest?
394. Can Roman numerals (X, M, V etc.) express all the numbers?
395. With which instrument can you measure the intensity of pain?
396. Which is the most prestigious science journal in the world?
397. Which gas did the chemical plant in Bhopal release to cause disaster on a large scale?
398. Which isotopes were required to make the atomic bomb?
399. Which book first propounded the concept of appropriate technology, i.e., technology suitable for the environment?
400. What is a microsecond?

9
ARTS AND CRAFTS

401. What kind of ware is Sheraton?

381. Mega
382. Metre/kilogramme/second
383. Phosphoric acid
384. Nitrous oxide
385. Lawrencium
386. Hydrogen
387. Lettuce (Pronounced 'letis')
388. RAdio Direction And Ranging
389. Analytic engine
390. The very heavy weight of the batteries
391. Bauxite
392. Fungi
393. Lithium
394. No, not zero
395. Algometer
396. *Nature*
397. Methyl isocyanate
398. Uranium-235 and Plutonium-239
399. *Small Is Beautiful*, by E.F. Schumacher
400. One millionth of a second

9
ANSWERS

401. Furniture. 18th century English

402. What are the Elgin Marbles and where are they to be found?

403. In which field of art did Rudolf Nureyev distinguish himself?

404. For how many years had Mozart been composing when he died at the age of thirty-five?

405. Which symphony of Beethoven is known as the *Eroica*?

406. Name the only opera composed by Beethoven.

407. Who directed the film *Hiroshima mon amour*?

408. Which was the first feature film made by Charlie Chaplin?

409. Who made the film *Viridiana*?

410. By what pseudonym was Charles Edouard Jeanneret known?

411. Who directed *2001: A Space Odyssey*?

412. What is the *Blue Danube*?

413. Which is the most frequently performed opera at the Royal Opera House, Covent Garden?

414. Who painted the famous portrait *La Gioconda*?

415. Who was the composer of the longest operas (the first six among the top ten)?

416. Who directed the film *La dolce vita*?

417. Who painted a series of water lilies in his own garden at Giverny?

418. Whose painting led to the term 'action painting'?

419. Which famous painting inspired W.H. Auden's poem 'Musee des Beaux Arts'?

420. Who painted *Guernica*, in condemnation of the Fascist bombing of that little town in the Spanish Civil War?

421. Who painted the ceiling of the Sistine Chapel in Rome?

422. Where is the Hermitage Museum, one of the world's foremost houses of art with over 8000 paintings of the Flemish, French, Dutch, Spanish, and Italian Schools?

402. Ancient Greek sculpture taken away by Lord Elgin from the temple of Athena at Acropolis in Athens and sold to the British Museum, where they are housed
403. Ballet dancing. He partnered Dame Margot Fonteyn
404. Thirty
405. The Third
406. *Fidelio*
407. Alain Resnais
408. *The Kid*
409. Luis Bunuel
410. Le Corbusier, architect
411. Stanley Kubrick
412. Waltz composed by Johann Strauss
413. Bizet's *Carmen*
414. Leonardo da Vinci; this is the other name of *Mona Lisa*
415. Richard Wagner (His *Goetterdaemmerung* is six hours long)
416. Frederico Fellini
417. Claude Monet
418. Jackson Pollock (He vigorously drew or 'dripped' complicated linear rhythms onto enormous canvases)
419. *The Fall of Icarus* by Pieter Bruegel
420. Pablo Picasso
421. Michelangelo Buonarroti (1475-1564)
422. Leningrad. Catherine II built it.

423. Who played the lead female role in the film *Yesterday, Today and Tomorrow*?

424. Which museum will you have to visit to see Leonardo da Vinci's *Mona Lisa*?

425. From which State do the magnificent bronze castings of Shiva (including the *Nataraja*) come?

426. Where is the lion capital on a Mauryan pillar from which the Government of India's seal is taken?

427. Where will you find the colossal rock sculpture, *The Descent of Ganga*?

428. In which museum would you find the famous statue of the Yakshi of Didarganj?

429. For which time of the day is *Raga Bhairavi* suitable for playing?

430. Which is the earliest Indian authority on the three arts, drama, music and dancing?

431. Which is the most ancient musical instrument of India?

432. What is the hand-gesture, the most striking feature of Indian dance, called?

433. Which dynasty of kings built the group of temples at Khajuraho?

434. Which temple building style does the Meenakshi Temple at Madurai represent?

435. Which is the finest example of Chola temple architecture?

436. Which is the most famous temple of the Pallava dynasty?

437. Which place is famous for its stylized terracotta horses?

438. In which States did the following dance forms originate: Kathakali, Bharat Natyam, Kuchipudi?

439. Which Indian musician's recording was introduced by Yehudi Menuhin?

440. To which school of classical vocal music did Ustad Abdul Karim Khan belong?

423. Sophia Loren
424. The Louvre, Paris
425. Tamil Nadu
426. Sarnath, in Bihar
427. Mamallapuram (Mahabalipuram)
428. The Patna Museum
429. Morning
430. Bharata's *Natyashastra*
431. The *Vina*
432. *Mudra*
433. The Chandellas
434. The Pandyan style
435. The temple of Shiva at Thanjavur (Tanjore)
436. The shore temple at Mamallapuram
437. Bankura in West Bengal
438. Kerala, Tamil Nadu, Andhra Pradesh
439. Ali Akbar Khan; sarod recording of Sindh Bhairavi and Pilu
440. The Kirana Gharana

441. To which school of light classical music did Rasoolan Bai belong?
442. Which is the oldest form of composition of Hindustani vocal classical music?
443. Which was Satyajit Ray's first film?
444. Where are the headquarters of the National Film Archive of India, established in 1964?
445. Who made the film *Do Bigha Zamin*?
446. In which film did Raj Kapoor make his debut?
447. India's first feature film was produced in 1913 by Dadasaheb Phalke. Can you name the film?
448. Through which film did sound come into Indian films?
449. In which field, other than nuclear science, has Dr. Raja Ramanna distinguished himself?
450. Who are the three outstanding composers of classical Carnatic music?

10

SPORTS

451. When did the Wimbledon Championship start?
452. How many teams play in the World Cup football?
453. To which country does the football club Benefica belong?
454. Who is the 'Kaiser' of West German football?
455. How is Graeco-Roman wrestling different from freestyle wrestling?
456. What is the normal playing time of a hockey match?
457. Which is the topmost grade in Judo?
458. When was the first World Amateur Snooker Championship held?
459. What are the Stoke Mandeville Games?

441. Banaras
442. Dhrupad
443. *Pather Panchali* (The Song of the Road)
444. Pune
445. Bimal Roy
446. *Neel Kamal*
447. *Raja Harishchandra*
448. *Alam Ara*
449. He is a gifted pianist as well
450. Thyagaraja, Mutthuswami Dikshitar, and Swami Shastri

10
ANSWERS

451. 1887
452. 16
453. Portugal
454. Franz Beckenbauer
455. In Graeco-Roman wrestling holds are barred below the waist
456. 70 minutes
457. 12th Dan
458. 1963 (Calcutta)
459. Olympics for the paralysed

460. Gavaskar holds the record of making the highest number of runs in Test cricket. How many runs in all did he make?

461. How many Tests did Don Bradman play in all and how many runs did he make?

462. Which Test cricketer has hit four consecutive sixes in a Test match?

463. How many centuries has Sunil Gavaskar scored in first class cricket?

464. On which cricket ground were the first Test match and the first One-Day International played?

465. What is the highest Test score by any Indian?

466. Which is the second oldest golf club in the world?

467. Who has been India's greatest wrestler ever?

468. What is traditional Japanese wrestling called?

469. How long do the shoulders have to be held down on the mat to record a fall in wrestling?

470. What is the heaviest weight ever lifted by a man?

471. Who lifted this weight?

472. Vijay Amritraj reached the Davis Cup final in 1974. What happened then?

473. What is the Grand Slam?

474. How many Indians have won the Wimbledon Junior title so far?

475. Who is a scratch golfer?

476. Which was the most inglorious Olympic for Indian hockey?

477. Can you name the years when India was the hockey champion of the world?

478. In 1976 a gymnast was awarded for the first time a perfect score of 10 by the judges. Who?

479. Which is the oldest football club in India?

480. Which Indian team was the first to win the I.F.A. Shield?

481. Name the countries which have won the World Cup twice.

460. 10122
461. 52 Tests, 6996 runs
462. Kapil Dev at Lord's, 1990
463. 80
464. Melbourne (1877, 1971)
465. 236 not out (S.M. Gavaskar, against West Indies, Madras, 1983-84)
466. Royal Calcutta Club
467. Gama (Mian Ghulam Mohammad)
468. Sumo
469. Four seconds
470. 2.8 tons
471. Paul Anderson (1957) of the USA
472. He didn't play against South Africa and conceded walkover
473. Winning the following tournaments in the same season: Wimbledon, U.S. Open, French Open and Australian Open
474. Three; Ramanathan Krishnan, Ramesh Krishnan, Leander Paes
475. One who has a handicap of 0
476. Montreal Olympics 1976 (India finished 7th)
477. 1928-56
478. Nadia Comaneci (Romania)
479. Dalhousie (Calcutta, 1878)
480. Mohun Bagan (1911)
481. Argentina, Uruguay

482. Apart from Brazil, has any other country won the World Cup thrice?
483. The Jules Rimet Trophy for World Cup winners was lifted permanently by a team in 1970. Which team?
484. Can you name the oldest football club in the world?
485. Who has been the heaviest of heavyweight boxing champions?
486. How much money did Muhammad Ali earn from his 61 fights?
487. How many times did Muhammad Ali become the World Heavyweight Boxing Champion?
488. At what height is the ring, which holds the basket in basketball, fixed?
489. Which is the most famous professional basketball team in the USA?
490. In which country is basketball the national game?
491. Who won the All-England Badminton Championship in 1980?
492. Who ran the first mile under four minutes?
493. What distance has to be covered in a modern marathon?
494. What was the most upsetting event in the 1936 Olympics held in Nazi Germany?
495. When were women first admitted to the Olympic Games?
496. What do the five rings on the Olympic flag mean?
497. When were the Olympic Games restarted after a gap of 1500 years (almost)?
498. Between which dates were the ancient Olympic Games held in Greece?
499. An Olympic swimming champion distinguished himself in another role, that of a super-he-man. Who is he?

482. Italy (1934, 1938, 1982); West Germany (1954, 1974, 1990)
483. Brazil (by winning it in 1958, 1962 and 1970)
484. Sheffield Football Club (1855)
485. Primo Carnera (Italy), 23 stones (322 lb)
486. $ 69 million
487. Three times
488. 10 feet from the ground
489. Harlem Globetrotters
490. USA
491. Prakash Padukone
492. Roger Bannister (Oxford University)
493. 26 miles 385 yards
494. A non-Aryan, black at that, won four gold medals. Hitler was most upset by Jesse Owens' success.
495. Amsterdam Olympics, 1928
496. They represent the five continents
497. 1896
498. 776 B.C. to A.D. 394 (Have you noted that B.C. comes after the date, whereas A.D. comes before the date, at least in educated writing?)
499. Johnny Weismuller or Tarzan. Olympic gold 1924, 1928

500. Name the first swimming club established in India.

11

ENVIRONMENT

501. Which National Park in India is in the midst of a very large lake?
502. What is the locale of Rudyard Kipling's jungle stories?
503. Which country has been a nuclear-free zone since 1984?
504. Coal burning stoves kept in the bedroom in severe winter often kill the occupants. How?
505. Name the poisonous herbicide used by the USA in Vietnam to deny forest cover to the enemies but which in addition caused death to men and animals in large numbers:
506. Among Indian trees which is the most beneficial medically?
507. So far which dam's construction has caused the displacement of the largest number of people in the world?
508. What percentage of earth's water lies imprisoned in glaciers and icecaps?
509. Which animal has become extinct in India as a result of indiscriminate hunting?
510. What is acid rain?
511. Besides cultural pollution, what is your neighbour causing by turning on Doordarshan at the maximum volume?
512. Among household effluents which should not be discharged into the drainage system?
513. What is a biodegradable material?
514. Among household wastes which is the most common material which does not lend itself to biodegradation?

11
ANSWERS

501. Madhupur National Park, Manipur
502. Kanha
503. New Zealand
504. By releasing carbon monoxide gas
505. Agent Orange
506. Neem (not Eucalyptus; it depletes the subsoil water level)
507. Aswan High Dam in Egypt
508. 70
509. The Cheetah
510. Precipitation of rain, snow, sleet, and hail containing high levels of sulphuric or nitric acids
511. Noise pollution
512. Oil and oily substances, as they kill marine life by covering the water with a film
513. That which is capable of being decomposed by bacteria or other biological means
514. Plastic

515. Bodies are often thrown into the Ganga for sacred water burial. Which animal had to be introduced in its waters to dispose of the waste flesh?

516. Which animal has been adopted by the World Wide Fund for Nature as its mascot?

517. With which crop did the Green Revolution start?

518. When did the Green Revolution start in India?

519. Which book was primarily responsible for environment consciousness in man?

520. The effect on environment of which particular chemical did Rachel Carson discuss?

521. What is solid waste?

522. What does biosphere mean?

523. What is meant by an ecosystem?

524. Why isn't it such a good idea any more to use chromium-plated cutlery and utensils?

525. Which deadly particle released by a nuclear explosion has the longest life?

526. Before pollution control came into effect which river was Europe's industrial sewer?

527. The release of many gases contributes to the green-house effect. Whose contribution is the highest?

528. Which among the vehicles causes the least atmospheric pollution?

529. To which of these pollutions, air, water, soil, are more human illnesses due?

531. Which metal, ingested in small doses, accumulates in the system and causes a chronic disease?

532. What is the major pollution problem inhibiting the growth of the nuclear power industry?

533. What stands in the way of introducing air pollution control systems in homes and places of work?

534. What does the term strangelove ocean signify?

515. Turtle
516. The Giant Panda
517. High-yielding varieties of wheat
518. 1966
519. Rachel Carson: *Silent Spring* (1962)
520. DDT
521. Junked appliances and vehicles
522. The sumtotal of life on earth
523. A complex of ecological community and environment forming a functioning whole in nature
524. Chromium is carcinogenic, i.e., it may cause cancer
525. Plutonium-239 (It collects in bones and affects the production of white blood cells)
526. The Rhine
527. Carbon dioxide
528. Bicycle (not bullock carts; cattle release methane gas)
529. Water pollution
531. Lead
532. Nuclear waste disposal
533. They are very expensive to instal
534. A lifeless ocean after a great human insult, such as a nuclear holocaust

535. What does the widespread use of DDT in agriculture cause to the birds?

536. Which bird was killed in large numbers to give ladies feathers for their hats?

537. What is going to happen if the Greenhouse effect crosses the tolerable limit?

538. Which gas at different levels of the atmosphere acts as an enemy and a friend to life on earth?

539. Which part of the human body is most vulnerable to nuclear radiation?

540. Being solely dependent on chemicals in the air for its nutrition, which plants are used as atmospheric pollution monitors?

541. Which little creature, often despised by men, greatly improves soil texture, surface infiltration, and drainage of water?

542. Which country, when it introduced rabbits, didn't foresee that it would upset its ecological balance?

543. Which country has pledged to phase out its nuclear power stations by the year 2010?

544. What does nuclear winter mean?

545. What is the Gaia hypothesis?

546. What does ecological wisdom mean?

547. What is the Greenhouse effect?

548. What is supposed to happen when there is an eco-freeze?

549. Which discipline studies trees as individuals in relation to their environment?

550. What is a green belt?

12

THE HUMAN BODY

551. What is the function of the pancreas?

552. In cataract surgery what does the surgeon remove?

535. Thinner eggshells from eating contaminated grains
536. Egret
537. All the ice (70% of the earth's water) will melt and much of the earth will be inundated
538. At the lower levels ozone traps sun's heat and poses a danger; at the upper level it filters harmful radiations from the sun
539. Bone marrow
540. Lichens
541. Earthworm
542. Australia
543. Sweden
544. The great fall in temperature after a nuclear holocaust
545. That the earth is alive and functions as a super-organism (Hypothesis formulated by James Lovelock; in Greek mythology Gaia is the earth)
546. The realization that man is a part of, and not an owner of, nature
547. A process by which heat is trapped on the surface of the earth by atmospheric pollution
548. Ecological degradation is halted
549. Forest autecology
550. A zone of farmland, parks, and open country surrounding a city, often officially designated as such and preserved from urban development

12
ANSWERS

551. It secretes digestive juices and hormones
552. The lens

553. What is the food of the brain?

554. What is the name of cancerous disorders of blood-forming tissues like the bone marrow, lymphatics, and spleen?

555. Which human organ is the least affected by harmful radiation?

556. How is the brain function monitored?

557. Which is the major cholesterol producing site in the human body?

558. Which gland of the human body is placed next to the brain?

559. Which is a sarcoma?

560. What is the most common cause of death in diarrhoea and dysentery?

561. What is STD in medical parlance?

562. Which part of the human brain controls unconscious activities like breathing?

563. Which disease can be caused by prolonged and inordinate use of painkillers?

564. What disease is caused by an inadequate supply of oxygen to the heart?

565. What is the medical cure of cataract?

566. What is the other name of German measles?

567. What is the difference between hay fever and common cold?

568. How many teeth do children have before they fall off, to be replaced by a set of 32?

569. The cheapest and the most effective method of treating diarrhoea and dysentery is ORT. What is it?

570. Is bile, which emulsifies and absorbs fat, acidic or alkaline?

571. Which part of the human body is the platella?

572. Which vitamins are water soluble and their excess in the body can be expelled through urine?

573. What is Koch's disease?

553. Glucose
554. Leukemia
555. The brain
556. By electroencephalography
557. The liver
558. Pineal
559. A malignant tumour
560. Dehydration
561. A sexually transmitted disease
562. Medulla oblongata
563. Ulceration of the stomach
564. Ischaemia
565. There is no medical cure
566. Rubella
567. Hay fever is allergic
568. Twenty
569. Oral Rehydration Therapy
570. Alkaline
571. The kneecap
572. Vitamins B and C
573. Tuberculosis

574. Ultraviolet radiation is administered to manufacture a particular vitamin in the skin. Which?

575. Which drug is commonly given to patients suffering from hypochondria, i.e., imaginary illnesses?

576. What is a diuretic drug?

577. What are the four blood groups?

578. What is the medical rating of perfect vision?

579. Have pimples anything to do with masturbation?

580. What IQ should you have if you think you are a genius?

581. How many calories of food should one take if one is not a manual worker?

582. How much more weight than normal should one carry to be called a fat man?

583. What is the full term of a pregnancy?

584. At what intervals can one donate blood?

585. What is the normal body temperature in Centigrade?

586. How long after blood circulation stops does the brain die?

587. What proportion of the body's weight are the bones?

588. What is the weight of the adult brain?

589. Which blood group should one have to be able to receive the blood of any group?

590. What is the function of the molar teeth?

591. Which part of the human brain controls man's intelligence, memory, speech, and learning?

592. Which is the longest bone in the human body?

593. How many bones are there in the human skeleton?

594. Why is the use of iodized salt recommended?

595. How much urine does a normal human body produce in a day?

596. Who was the first Caesarean baby in medical history?

574. Vitamin D
575. Placebo (pronounced pla-ci-bo)
576. That which increases the flow of urine
577. O, A, B, AB
578. 6/6 (metres) or 20/20 (feet)
579. No. They are caused by hormonal imbalances
580. 140 and above
581. Between 1800 and 2000 calories
582. 20 kg. more than what he should weigh
583. 280 days/10 lunar months
584. Every three months
585. 37°C
586. 3 minutes
587. About 20%
588. 1-1.5 kg.
589. AB; people with this blood group are universal recipients
590. They chew and grind
591. The cerebrum
592. The femur or the thighbone
593. 206
594. For the proper functioning of the thyroid gland to prevent goitre, which is a swelling of the thyroid gland
595. 1.44 litres
596. Julius Caesar

597. What dangerous side effect can be caused by the administration of Streptomycin?
598. When is a baby called premature?
599. What is Hansen's disease?
600. Surgical male sterilization is vasectomy; what is surgical female sterilization?

13

INDIAN LITERATURE

601. Who received the first Sahitya Akademi award for English?
602. For which feature film did Satyajit Ray take a story from Prem Chand?
603. G.V. Desani published a novel in 1948 which was greeted with rare enthusiasm by T.S. Eliot and others. Can you name it?
604. Who wrote the much-performed English play *Tughlaq*?
605. The 1988 Sahitya Akademi award in Urdu was awarded to an eminent politician, posthumously. Can you name him?
606. What is the name of Raja Rao's collection of stories on the Ganga Ghat?
607. Who wrote the *Panchtantra* tales in Sanskrit?
608. *The Ramayana* is the national epic of the Tamils. Who wrote it?
609. Can you name Salman Rushdie's first novel?
610. Which distinguished poet named his autobiography *My Son's Father*?
611. Can you name the epic that Jaishankar Prasad wrote?
612. Mahatma Gandhi wrote an autobiography distinguished for its honesty and lack of evasion. What is it called?
613. Who wrote under the pen-name Ajneya?
614. Whose play is *Evam Indrajit* (And Indrajit)?

597. Deafness
598. When it is born four weeks or more before the 40th week
599. Leprosy
600. Tubectomy/Tube ligature (Also, Salpingectomy)

13
ANSWERS

601. R.K. Narayan
602. *Shatranj ke Khilari* (The Chess Players)
603. *All About H. Hatterr*
604. Girish Karnad
605. Sheikh Abdullah
606. *On the Ganga Ghat*
607. Vishnusharma
608. Kamban
609. *Grimus*
610. Dom Moraes
611. *Kamayani*
612. *My Experiments with Truth*
613. Satchitanand Hiranand Vatsayana
614. Badal Sirkar

615. Which dramatist wrote in Hindi the play *Aadhe-Aadhure* (chiaroscuro)

616. Which foreign poet is so far the only Honorary Fellow of the Sahitya Akademi

617. Who is the author of *So Many Hungers!*?

618. Which is the oldest surviving Sanskrit text on grammar?

619. For which book of poems was Rabindranath Tagore awarded the Nobel Prize in 1913?

620. Can you say what Manohar Malgonkar's *A Bend in the Ganges* is about?

621. Name the first Mulk Raj Anand novel to be published.

622. Who wrote the narrative poem *The Golden Gate* and took the American literary scene by storm?

623. Who was the first recipient of the Bharatiya Jnanpith award?

624. What is the Bharatiya Jnanpith award made for?

625. Which Indian poet wrote the much anthologized poem 'A Goodbye Party to Miss Pushpa T.S.' and 'The Night of the Scorpion'?

626. Which Indian author first went to England at the age of 57, and wrote *A Passage to England*?

627. Which was R.K. Narayan's first book?

628. In which language did the devotional poet Namdev write?

629. Which Hindi poet received the Sahitya Akademi as well as the Jnanpith awards?

630. To which Book of the *Mahabharata* does the *Geeta* belong?

631. In how many Books is the *Mahabharata* completed?

632. Who wrote *Ramacharitmanasa* — the holy lake of the acts of Rama?

633. To whom is the original *Mahabharata* ascribed?

634. Who composed the great Tamil epic, *Silappadikaram* (the bejewelled ankle)?

615. Mohan Rakesh
616. Leopold Segar Senghor
617. Bhabani Bhattacharya
618. Yaska's *Nirukta*
619. *Gitanjali* (Song Offerings)
620. The Sepoy Mutiny
621. *Untouchable*
622. Vikram Seth
623. G. Shankara Kurup, writing in Malayalam
624. The best creative writing by any Indian in any Indian language in the last twenty years
625. Nissim Ezekiel
626. Nirad C. Chaudhuri
627. *Swami and Friends*
628. Marathi
629. Sumitranandan Pant
630. Sixth
631. Eighteen
632. Tulasidasa
633. Ved Vyasa
634. Ilango Adigal

635. Who made the first English translation of Kalidasa's *Sakuntala* and when?
636. Who was the founder of Bharatiya Jnanpith?
637. Which major Indian writer in English has the Sahitya Akademi failed to honour so far?
638. Keki N. Daruwalla wrote a series of haunting poems on the Ganga at Varanasi. In which book of his can these be read?
639. What is Upamanyu Chatterjee's novel of total irreverence for the establishment called?
640. Many regard *Samskara* the most important novel written by an Indian in the last fifty years. Can you name the author and the English translator?
641. Amitav Ghosh is one the most significant novelists writing in English in the eighties. Can you name his novels?
642. How many Sahitya Akademi awards are made in all, one for each language?
643. Which is still the best dictionary of Anglo-Indian words in English?
644. Which was Kamala Markandeya's first novel?
645. One of Sudhin N. Ghose's novels, much admired by English critics (it was published in England and few copies reached India), is now available in a local reprint. Name the novel.
646. Whose first novel was *The Strange Case of Billy Biswas*?
647. Which short story writer, who settled in Pakistan and died there in 1955, is regarded as one of the most powerful writers in the Indian subcontinent?
648. For which among the following films is Satyajit Ray indebted to Tagore's stories: (a) *Teen Kanya* (b) *Charulata* (c) *Ghare Baire* (d) *Pather Panchali*?
649. Who wrote the national song *Bande Mataram*, second only in importance to *Janaganamana*?
650. Who wrote India's national anthem *Janaganamana*?

635. Sir William Jones; 1789
636. Sahu S.P. Jain
637. Khushwant Singh
638. *Crossing of Rivers*
639. *English, August*
640. U.R. Anantha Murthy; translated from Kannada by A.K. Ramanujan
641. *The Circle of Reason* and *The Shadow Lines*
642. 22
643. *Hobson-Jobson*
644. *Nectar in a Sieve*
645. *The Vermilion Boat*
646. Arun Joshi
647. Saadat Hasan Manto
648. (a), (b), (c)
649. Bankim Chandra Chatterji, in his novel *Anandamath*
650. Rabindranath Tagore

14

WORLD LITERATURE

651. What is the nationality of the Nobel Prize-winning African author, Wole Soyinka?
652. In which language were the plays of Henrik Ibsen originally written?
653. Which famous English poet was drowned?
654. Which famous English poet was born American?
655. Name two famous British authors who were born in India:
656. About whom did Abraham Lincoln say that the little woman's book made the American Civil War?
657. Who was the first person to receive the Nobel Prize for Literature?
658. When did the first batch of Penguin Books come out?
659. An Agatha Christie story, dramatized, had a run of more than 10,000 nights in London. Name the play.
660. A noted philosopher and novelist refused the Nobel Prize for Literature 1964, the only one to do so. Who?
661. Dr. Johnson was not only a good poet and critic, he was also a brilliant conversationalist. Which famous book records his conversations?
662. In which book do we find an account of the noble, rational horses, and ignoble, irrational men?
663. The fable of the clever cock and the fox has been told by Chaucer in a narrative poem. What is its name?
664. In which play of Shakespeare is Olivia a character?
665. Which play of Shakespeare is set in Elsinore in Denmark?

14
ANSWERS

651. Nigerian
652. Norwegian
653. Percy Bysshe Shelley
654. T.S. Eliot
655. 1. W.M. Thackeray 2. Rudyard Kipling
     3. George Orwell
656. Harriet Beecher Stowe. The book is *Uncle Tom's Cabin*
657. R.F.A. Sully-Prudhomme
658. 1935
659. *The Mousetrap*
660. Jean-Paul Sartre
661. Boswell's *Life of Johnson*
662. *Gulliver's Travels*, by Jonathan Swift, Book Four
663. *The Nun's Priest's Tale*
664. Twelfth Night
665. Hamlet

666. Who is the scholars' favourite candidate for *really* writing Shakespeare's plays?

667. When was the first complete, standard edition of Shakespeare's plays published? Shakespeare died in 1616.

668. How many plays did Shakespeare write?

669. Which novel established Kingsley Amis's reputation?

670. Of which comic and bawdy novel of J.P. Donleavy is Alec Sebastian Dangerfield the unheroic hero?

671. In which famous detective story is the narrator himself the murderer?

672. Who wrote *The Secret Diary of Adrian Mole Aged 13¾,* which for a long time remained on the bestseller list?

673. In which novel is Barkis willin'?

674. Who is the Lord of the Flies in William Golding's novel of the same name?

675. Who was the most celebrated Pole who was an important English novelist?

676. Whose aged relative is Aunt Agatha?

677. In whose novel does Rose Stanley (famous for sex) appear?

678. In which novel does the character of Saleem Sinai appear?

679. Who wrote the long poem *Troilus and Criseyde?*

680. Who is the spy in John Le Carré's *Tinker, Tailor, Soldier, Spy?*

681. Who hid in an apple barrel and heard a conspiracy?

682. Can you name H.R.F. Keating's Indian detective?

683. Who are the authors of two novels with the same name, *Justine?*

684. Which is John Le Carré's first book?

685. In which children's classic does Passepartout the servant appear?

666. Bacon
667. 1623
668. 36, plus a considerable part of *Pericles*
669. *Lucky Jim*
670. *The Ginger Man*
671. *The Murder of Roger Ackroyd;* Agatha Christie
672. Sue Townsend
673. *David Copperfield;* Charles Dickens
674. Beelzebub
675. Joseph Conrad
676. Bertie Wooster's; P.G. Wodehouse character
677. *The Prime of Miss Jean Brodie*, by Muriel Spark
678. *Midnight's Children* by Salman Rushdie
679. Geoffrey Chaucer
680. Bill Haydon
681. Jim Hawkins in Stevenson's *Treasure Island*
682. Inspector Ghote
683. Marquis de Sade and Lawrence Durrell
684. *Call for the Dead*
685. *Around the World in Eighty Days*

686. 'The more perfect the artist, the more complete-
     ly separate in him will be the man who suffers
     and the mind which creates.' — Which modern
     poet and critic said that?
687. Which play did Arthur Miller write for his wife
     Marylin Monroe?
688. In which modern play will you meet Estragon,
     Vladimir, Lucky, and Pozzo?
689. With which play did Henrik Ibsen made his
     name as a sensational new dramatist?
690. Who wrote *Desire under the Elms* which was made
     into a film with Sophia Loren in the female lead
     role?
691. Who wrote *Murder in the Cathedral*, a verse
     drama on the martyrdom of Thomas Becket?
692. When Paris ran away with Helen who was her
     husband?
693. In Greek literature a man killed his father and
     unknowingly married his mother. Who is he?
694. Which novel is considered to be the mirror of
     the Jazz Age in America?
695. Name the cigar-smoking American poetess.
696. In which book does Aldous Huxley write about
     his travels in India?
697. Which Japanese novelist committed ritual
     suicide in 1972 after haranguing Japan's army
     for its impotence?
698. What is James Hadley Chase's real name?
699. Which Russian author now writes his novels in
     the most distinguished English?
700. Which Nobel Prize-winning author wrote *One
     Hundred Years of Solitude?*

686. T.S. Eliot
687. *The Misfits*
688. *Waiting for Godot* by Samuel Beckett
689. *An Enemy of the People*
690. Eugene O'Neill
691. T.S. Eliot
692. Menelaus
693. King Oedipus
694. *The Great Gatsby* by F. Scott-Fitzgerald
695. Amy Lowell
696. *Jesting Pilate*
697. Yukio Mishima
698. René Raymond
699. Vladimir Nabokov
700. Gabriel Garcia Marquez

15
FACTS ABOUT INDIA

701. Which State of India has kept population most under control?
702. Where is the Indian Institute of Advanced Study (still) located?
703. When was the first college in India, Hindu College, Calcutta (later Presidency College), founded?
704. When was press censorship first introduced in India?
705. Which is the most literate State in India?
706. Which campaigner for widow remarriage matched precept with practice by giving his son in marriage to a widow?
707. What was India's literacy rate at the last census in 1981?
708. What was India's total population according to the 1981 census?
709. Which was the first newspaper in India and who edited it?
710. Which are the largest and smallest States in India areawise?
711. How much of India's petroleum needs has to be imported?
712. Which Indian State is the least electrified?
713. What is the percentage of the educated un-employed to the total unemployed in the country? (1981 census)
714. On which river has the Hirakud Dam been built?
715. How many Indian languages are recognized by the Eighth Schedule of the Constitution?

15
ANSWERS

701. Tamil Nadu
702. Shimla; at the old Viceregal lodge
703. 1817
704. Effectively, in 1782, when Warren Hastings suppressed Hicky's *Bengal Gazette*
705. Kerala
706. Pandit Ishwar Chandra Vidyasagar
707. 36.2%
708. 685 million
709. *Bengal Gazette* 1880; William Hicky
710. Madhya Pradesh and Goa
711. 30%
712. Arunachal Pradesh
713. 46.8
714. Mahanadi
715. 15

716. China is a little more than three times the size of India, and yet its population is only 1.47 times greater. What is their relative density of population per sq km?

717. What is the other name of the Great Indian Desert?

718. When did the first partition of Bengal take place?

719. Who was the first president of the Indian National Congress session at Bombay in 1885?

720. What is China's population?

721. Which is India's oldest shipbuilding yard?

722. When did the British Crown take over the government of India from the East India Company?

723. Which is the largest port in India?

724. Which regiment was involved in the outbreak of the Mutiny in Meerut on 10 May 1857?

725. Which Indian State leads in the number of factories?

726. Which State in India has the largest number of hospitals?

727. When was rationing first introduced in India?

728. How many kilometres of tracks do the Indian Railways have?

729. When was the Planning Commission set up in India?

730. Which State in India has all the villages connected by all-weather roads?

731. Which is the longest of the long distance trains running in India?

732. When was the first indigenous railway engine built at the Chittaranjan Locomotive Works?

733. Who holds the record for taking the maximum number of his wives (concubines not included) to his funeral pyre?

734. Of the 17,000 or so books published in India what is the percentage of children's books?

716. China 105.43: India 214
717. Thar Desert
718. 1905
719. W.C. Bonnerjea
720. 1008 million
721. Visakhapatnam
722. 1858
723. Bombay
724. The Third Native Cavalry
725. Maharashtra
726. Kerala
727. 1943, during the great famine in Bengal
728. 62,000
729. 1950
730. Kerala
731. Guwahati-Trivandrum Express
732. 1950
733. The Raja of Marwar, 64 wives, 1780
734. 1.2%

735. When did the railway train make its debut in India?

736. What were the English names of the five rivers of Punjab: Shatadru, Bipasha, Irawati, Chandrabhaga, and Vitasta?

737. According to the 1981 census how many Senior Citizens (age 60+) are there in India?

738. Which State in India has the largest tribal population? Verrier Elwin worked here.

739. What is the distance between India's northernmost and southernmost tips?

740. Who is the father of the chemical industry in India?

741. Which constitutional amendment froze the number of Lok Sabha seats to 545 till the end of the year 2000?

742. When was the Indian National Congress split for the first time after independence?

743. In which year was the Communist Party of India founded?

744. Which is the most populous city in India?

745. Which are the two least urbanized States in India?

746. When did the Jallianwala Bagh massacre take place?

747. In which year did Mahatma Gandhi return from South Africa to take part in the Indian freedom movement?

748. In which Five Year Plan did energy and power receive the highest allocation of funds?

749. Which State in India is most urbanized?

750. Which three persons took an active part in the abolition of the suttee in 1829?

735. 1853
736. Sutlej, Beas, Ravi, Chenab, and Jhelum
737. 43 million
738. Madhya Pradesh
739. 3214 km
740. P.C. Ray; he founded the Bengal Chemical and Pharmaceutical Works in 1901
741. The 42nd Amendment
742. 1969
743. 1925
744. Calcutta (9.2 million)
745. Himachal Pradesh and Arunachal Pradesh
746. 13 April 1919
747. 1915
748. The Seventh Five Year Plan
749. Maharashtra
750. Raja Rammohun Roy, Charles Metcalfe, and William Bentinck

16
GEOGRAPHY

751. Which is the river up which ocean-going ships can go to 3700 km?
752. From the mines of which country do 90% of the emeralds of the world come?
753. Where is the Pitch Lake, an inexhaustible lake of asphalt, located?
754. What is generally considered to be the boundary between North and South America?
755. Which State did the United States buy from Russia in 1867 for $72,000,000?
756. In which State of Africa are the Victoria Falls located?
757. Which is the safariland of Africa?
758. Which is Africa's most populous country?
759. Which country of the world produces the most cocoa?
760. In which country of the world has the earth's highest surface temperature, 57.7°C, been recorded?
761. Which country of the world consists of more than 13,000 islands?
762. In which country of the world is oil more plentiful than water?
763. Name the capital of North Korea.
764. Which is the world's most severely typhoon-hit region?
765. Where is the winter coldest among the populated spots of the world?
766. Which is the world's deepest depression?
767. From which country's original name was the word copper derived?
768. Which country is Europe's fruit and vegetable garden?

16
ANSWERS

751. Amazon (ships can go up to Iquitos, Brazil)
752. Colombia
753. Trinidad
754. The Isthmus of Panama
755. Alaska
756. Zambia
757. Kenya
758. Nigeria (82.39 million)
759. Ivory Coast
760. Al Aziziyah in Libya
761. Indonesia
762. Bahrain
763. Pyongyang
764. South China Sea
765. North-eastern Siberia (below −50°C)
766. The Dead Sea in the Jordan valley; -402m
767. Cyprus (original name Kypros)
768. Bulgaria

769. Which country produces the cork for every second wine bottle in the world?

770. Which capital city in Europe is divided by the Danube?

771. What is the capital of the EEC?

772. In which country does more than one-third of the land lie below the sea level?

773. How much of the USSR is considered to be in Asia and what percentage of its population lives there?

774. In which country does the world's oldest company, Stora, chartered in 1280, still mine copper?

775. What percentage of agricultural land covers Europe?

776. Which is Europe's longest river?

777. Which country is called a Land of Thousand Lakes, although a hundred thousand lakes would be a more correct description?

778. Which two countries does the traditional boundary line between Europe and Asia divide?

779. Which is Europe's highest active volcano which erupted as late as 1984?

780. Where has Europe's highest temperature, 51°C, been recorded?

781. Which is Europe's largest island?

782. In which modern State do the ancient cities of Nineveh and Babylon fall?

783. Dispute over navigational rights in one particular waterways was the main cause of Iraq-Iran war (1980-90). Name the waterways and the ports which command it.

784. Which country can you enter either through the Caspian Sea or the Persian Gulf?

785. The Tropic of Cancer and the Tropic of Capricorn are the same latitude North and South. What is it?

769. Portugal
770. Budapest
771. Brussels
772. Netherlands
773. 75% and 25%
774. Sweden
775. 40%; the highest among all continents
776. Volga (3690 km)
777. Finland
778. USSR and Turkey
779. Mt. Etna in Sicily (3340m)
780. Seville, Spain
781. Britain
782. Iraq
783. Shatt al Arab Waterways; Al Basrah(Iraq) and Abadan (Iran)
784. Iran
785. 23.5°

786. Where in the world has the lowest air temperature been recorded?
787. How much of the earth is covered by sea?
788. Which is by far the largest desert of the world?
789. Which is the second largest desert in the world, and how much smaller is it than the largest?
790. Which is the world's largest island, 2.68 times larger than the next largest, New Guinea?
791. Which area of the world has the largest number of volcanic mountains?
792. Which is the world's widest waterfall?
793. Which is the world's highest waterfall, measured from lip to base?
794. Which is the world's largest canal system?
795. Which is the second largest river in the world?
796. Which is the deepest known lake in the world?
797. Which is the world's largest sweetwater lake?
798. Which is the world's largest natural saltwater lake?
799. The largest ocean in the world is the Pacific and the next is the Atlantic. How much larger is the former?
800. What is the height of the second highest mountain of the world? Give its two names.

17

QUOTES

801. Who said, 'Punctuality is the politeness of kings'?
802. 'Genius is one per cent inspiration and ninety-nine per cent perspiration' — who is the father of this advice freely handed out to lazy children?
803. Who wrote, 'No man is an Island, entire of itself ... Any man's death diminishes me, because I am involved in Mankind; And therefore never send to know for whom the bell tolls; It tolls for thee'?

786. Vostok (−88.3°C) on the Antarctica Polar Plateau
787. 70.92%
788. Sahara in North Africa (8,400,000 sq km)
789. Gobi, in Mongolia. It is only 15.4% of the Sahara, its area being 1,295,000 sq km
790. Greenland (2,130,265 sq km)
791. Japan and Taiwan (On an average Tokyo is shaken by an earthquake once every week)
792. Khone (10,800m; Laos)
793. Angel Falls (979m; Venezuela)
794. The Volga-Baltic Canal System (2300 km)
795. Amazon (6570 km)
796. Lake Baikal (maximum known depth 5714 ft or 1742 m)
797. Lake Superior (82,350 sq km)
798. The Caspian Sea (360,700 sq km)
799. 2.01 times; 165,384,000 sq km: 82,217,000 sq km
800. 8611m; K2 or Godwin-Austen

17
ANSWERS

801. Louis XVIII (1755-1824)
802. Thomas Alva Edison (1847-1931)
803. John Donne (1572-1631)

804. 'Beware that you do not lose the substance by grasping at the shadow' — whose warning is this?

805. Which journalist said, 'Comment is free, but facts are sacred'?

806. Whose novel begins with this sentence: 'It is a truth universally acknowledged that a single man in possession of a good fortune, must be in want of a wife'?

807. Who said, 'Man is by nature a political animal'?

808. Which philosopher said, 'Those who cannot remember the past are condemned to repeat it'?

809. Who had this note on his Presidential desk: 'The buck stops here'?

810. Who said, 'Power tends to corrupt, and absolute power corrupts absolutely'?

811. Who said, 'Anybody who goes to see a psychiatrist ought to have his head examined'?

812. Who observed, 'The dullard's envy of brilliant men is always assuaged by the suspicion that they will come to a bad end'?

813. Which film director said, 'Every film should have a beginning, a middle and an end — but not necessarily in that order'?

814. Which industrial magnate said, 'History is more or less all bunk'?

815. Who said, 'Whom God would destroy He first makes mad'?

816. 'Never in the field of human conflict was so much owed by so many to so few' — who paid this moving tribute to the RAF Fighter Command in World War II?

817. Who said, 'There's a sucker born every minute'?

818. 'When in Rome, live as the Romans do; when elsewhere live as they live elsewhere' — whose advice is this?

804. Aesop, in his fable 'The Dog and the Shadow'
805. C.P. Scott (1846-1932), British journalist
806. Jane Austen, *Pride and Prejudice*
807. Aristotle (384-322 B.C.)
808. George Santayana (1863-1952)
809. U.S. President Harry S. Truman (1884-1972)
810. Lord Acton (1834-1902)
811. Samuel Goldwin of MGM (1882-1974)
812. Max Beerbohm (1872-1956)
813. Jean-Luc Godard (b. 1930)
814. Henry Ford (1863-1947)
815. Euripides (480-406 B.C.)
816. Winston Churchill (1874-1965) in the House of Commons, 20 August 1940
817. Phineas T. Barnum of Barnum's Circus
818. St. Ambrose, Bishop of Milan (*c.* 339-397)

819. Who said, 'You can fool all the people some of the time, and some of the people all the time, but you cannot fool all the people all the time'?

820. Which scientist said, 'Give me a firm place to stand, and I will move the earth'?

821. Which politician said, 'I would rather be an opportunist and float than go to the bottom with my principles round my neck'?

822. Which statesman said, 'The greater the lie, the greater the chance that it will be believed'?

823. Who wrote, 'There is in human nature generally more of the fool than of the wise'?

824. Who said about his fighting technique, 'Float like a butterfly, sting like a bee'?

825. About whom was this catchphrase widely used: 'Would you buy a used car from this man'?

826. Which famous conductor said, 'The English may not like music — but they absolutely love the noise it makes'?

827. Who made the statement, 'A house is a machine for living in'?

828. Who is this attributed to (means that even *he* couldn't have said it really): 'You have tasted two whole worms; you have hissed all my mystery lectures and have been caught fighting a liar in the quad; you will have to leave by the next town drain'?

829. Who said, 'Superstition is the religion of feeble minds'?

830. Which eminent jurist said, 'It is better that ten guilty persons escape than one innocent suffer'?

831. Who said, 'The remarkable thing about Shakespeare is that he is really very good — in spite of all the people who say he is very good'?

832. Who said, 'We are all strong enough to bear the misfortunes of others'?

833. Who wrote 'Human kind
                    Cannot bear very much reality'?

819. Abraham Lincoln (1809-1865)
820. Archimedes (287-212 B.C.)
821. Stanley Baldwin (1867-1947)
822. Adolf Hitler (1889-1945)
823. Francis Bacon (1561-1626)
824. Muhammad Ali, the boxer (b. 1942)
825. Richard M. Nixon (b. 1913)
826. Sir Thomas Beecham (1879-1971)
827. Le Corbusier (1887-1965), French architect
828. William Archibald Spooner (1844-1930)
829. Edmund Burke (1729-1797)
830. Sir William Blackstone (1723-1780)
831. Robert Graves (1895-1985)
832. La Rochefoucauld (1613-1680)
833. T.S. Eliot, in *Burnt Norton*

834. Who said, 'There is no such thing as a moral or an immoral book. Books are well written, or badly written'?

835. Who called patriotism the last refuge of a scoundrel?

836. Who said, 'Every man over forty is a scoundrel'?

837. Who defined a bore as 'a person who talks when you wish him to listen'?

838. Who wrote, 'A spectre is haunting Europe — the spectre of Communism'?

839. Who said on the eve of World War I, 'The lamps are going out all over Europe: we shall not see them lit again in our lifetime'?

840. Who defined a cynic as a man who knows the price of everything and the value of nothing?

841. Which British novelist said, 'The proper study of mankind is books'?

842. Who said, 'I disapprove of what you say, but I will defend to the death your right to say it'?

843. Who said, 'That's one small step for a man, one giant leap for humanity'?

844. Which mountaineer, when asked why he wanted to climb Mount Everest, said, 'Because it is there'?

845. 'It's a recession when your neighbour loses his job; it's a depression when you lose your own' — which statesman said this?

846. Who first said, '*Vox populi, vox dei*', the voice of the people is the voice of God?

847. Who defined peace as 'a period of cheating between two periods of fighting'?

848. Who is the following attributed to: 'Everything should be made as simple as possible, but not simpler'?

849. Who said this of the middle-of-the-roaders, 'We know what happens to people who stay in the middle of the road. They get run over'?

834. Oscar Wilde (1854-1900)
835. Samuel Johnson (1709-1784)
836. George Bernard Shaw (1856-1950)
837. Ambrose Bierce (1842-1914) in *The Devil's Dictionary*
838. Karl Marx (1818-1883), in *The Communist Manifesto*
839. Viscount Grey of Fallodon (1862-1933)
840. Oscar Wilde (1854-1900)
841. Aldous Huxley (1894-1963)
842. Voltaire (1694-1778)
843. Neil Armstrong, on stepping down on the moon's surface, 20 July 1969
844. George Leigh Mallory (1886-1924)
845. Harry S. Truman (1884-1972), U.S. President
846. Bishop Alcuin (735-804)
847. Ambrose Bierce (1842-1914 when last seen)
848. Albert Einstein (1879-1955)
849. Aneurin Bevan (1897-1960)

850. What is this known as: 'If anything can go wrong it will'?

18

WORDPOWER

Choose the correct antonym

851. Amity: (a) Disunity (b) Enmity (c) Competition (d) Harmony
852. Dilatory: (a) Quick (b) Loitering (c) Diluted (d) Straightforward
853. Indigent: (a) Native (b) Foreign (c) Rich (d) Careful
854. Ambivalent: (a) Bivalent (b) Unclear (c) Clear (d) Rich
855. Affluent: (a) Divided (b) Rich (c) Poor (d) Confluent
856. Temporal: (a) Eternal (b) Permanent (c) Placid (d) Spiritual
857. Myopic: (a) Astigmatic (b) Farsighted (c) Clearsighted (d) Realistic
858. Risible: (a) Calm (b) Serious (c) Fallible (d) Sweet-tempered
859. Bracing: (a) Loose (b) Indisciplined (c) Constricting (d) Enervating
860. Pollute: (a) Improve (b) Strengthen (c) Beautify (d) Purify
861. Ingenuous: (a) Unskilful (b) Sly (c) Clumsy (d) Unoriginal
862. Diabolical: (a) Beautiful (b) Merciful (c) Divine (d) Angelic
863. Pragmatic: (a) Unpractical (b) Inexperienced (c) Theoretic (d) Ideal
864. Belligerent: (a) Timid (b) Bashful (c) Nonviolent (d) Peaceful
865. Lugubrious: (a) Steady (b) Comely (c) Gay (d) Well-mannered

18
ANSWERS

851. (b)
852. (a)
853. (c)
854. (c)
855. (c)
856. (d)
857. (b)
858. (b)
859. (d)
860. (d)
861. (b)
862. (c)
863. (c)
864. (d)
865. (c)

866. Wanton: (a) Chaste (b) Civilized (c) Moral (d) Controlled
867. Figment: (a) Wholeness (b) Fact (c) Reality (d) Invention
868. Exacerbate: (a) Ameliorate (b) Belittle (c) Embitter (d) Soothe
869. Vulnerable: (a) Secure (b) Strong (c) Doubting (d) Invincible
870. Germane: (a) Irrelevant (b) Contradictory (c) Improbable (d) Imaginary
871. Geriatric: (a) Mature (b) Youthful (c) Naive (d) Kind
872. Haughty: (a) Humble (b) Reasonable (c) Kindly (d) Sweet-tempered
873. Piquant: (a) Dull (b) Tasteless (c) Mild (d) Gentle
874. Specious: (a) Narrow (b) Reasonable (c) Genuine (d) Right
875. Bull: (a) Ox (b) Buffalo (c) Cow (d) Bear

Choose the correct synonym

876. Absolve: (a) Punish (b) Dilute (c) Complicate (d) Acquit
877. Doughty: (a) Brave (b) Fat (c) Strong (d) Fierce
878. Immaculate: (a) Illegitimate (b) Holy (c) Impure (d) Clean
879. Mendacious: (a) Truthful (b) Lying (c) Compromising (d) Evil
880. Morbid: (a) Fearful (b) Obscene (c) Fervid (d) Sick
881. Menage: (a) Circus (b) Home (c) Zoo (d) Boarding house
882. Cortege: (a) Procession (b) Cart (c) Carriage for the dead (d) Decorated car
883. Obsequious: (a) Mournful (b) Sympathetic (c) Funeral (d) Servile
884. Mundane: (a) Day-to-day (b) Ordinary (c) Earthly (d) Material

866. (a)
867. (b)
868. (d)
869. (a)
870. (a)
871. (b)
872. (a)
873. (c)
874. (c)
875. (d) This one was a stock market bull
876. (d)
877. (a)
878. (d)
879. (b)
880. (d)
881. (b)
882. (a)
883. (d)
884. (c)

885. Sycophant: (a) Toady (b) Helpful (c) Servile (d) Eager
886. Propitious: (a) Timely (b) Favourable (c) Appropriate (d) Fortunate
887. Maladroit: (a) Wrong (b) Inappropriate (c) Clumsy (d) Ill-timed
888. Pussilanimous: (a) Eager to fight (b) Cowardly (c) Energetic (d) Powerful
889. Corporeal: (a) Military (b) Related to a company (c) Earthly (d) Physical
890. Chary: (a) Cautious (b) Reluctant (c) Unwilling (d) Hostile
891. Contumely: (a) Immediately (b) Appropriately (c) Humility (d) Arrogance
892. Factious: (a) Quarrelsome (b) Intriguing (c) Bad tempered (d) Irritable
893. Insidious: (a) Complicated (b) Complex (c) Deceitful (d) Vague
894. Improbity: (a) Dishonesty (b) Impossibility (c) Unlikelihood (d) Uncertainty
895. Recondite: (a) Learned (b) Difficult (c) Outdated (d) Obscure
896. *Amour propre:* (a) True love (b) Platonic love (c) Self-love (d) Chaste love
897. Turgid: (a) Swollen (b) Muddy (c) Impure (d) Rotting
898. Querulous: (a) Quarrelsome (b) Complaining (c) Nagging (d) Dissatisfied
899. Purview: (a) Examination (b) Jurisdiction (c) Scope (d) Overview
900. Insouciant: (a) Smart (b) Unrepentant (c) Suave (d) Unconcerned

885. (a)
886. (b)
887. (c)
888. (b)
889. (d)
890. (a)
891. (d)
892. (d)
893. (c)
894. (a)
895. (d)
896. (c)
897. (a)
898. (b)
899. (c)
900. (d)

19

MATTERS OF MIND

901. What is the meaning of the Greek word 'philosophy'?
902. Who left a written account of the last days and death of Socrates?
903. What is Platonic love?
904. Which philosophical system did Karl Marx propound?
905. What is the concept of animism?
906. Who were Sigmund Freud's associates in Vienna in his psychiatric work?
907. Who was the first to advance the heliocentric theory of the universe, i.e., that the earth and the planets revolve round the sun?
908. What was the Philosopher's Stone much sought after in medieval times?
909. What is Oedipus Complex?
910. Who was Oedipus in Greek myth and what did he do?
911. What is hedonism in the ethical context?
912. Who postulated the concept of the collective unconscious?
913. What is a totem?
914. Who developed the philosophy of Christian existentialism?
915. What is the essence of Socratic dialogue as a method of teaching?
916. Which school of philosophy did Shankara (A.D. 788-820) found?
917. Who is the author of *A History of Western Philosophy*?
918. What is epistemology about?

ANSWERS

901. Love of wisdom
902. Plato
903. Love free from physical desire
904. Dialectical materialism
905. That a spirit or force resides in every animate or inanimate object
906. C.G. Jung and Alfred Adler
907. Aristarchus of Samos (310-230 B.C.)
908. A substance that would turn base metals into gold
909. Childhood hostility towards the parent of the same sex and attraction towards the parent of the opposite sex
910. Son of King Laius of Thebes and Queen Jocasta, he was abandoned on a mountainside following a prophecy that he would kill his father. On growing up, on his way to Thebes, he met, quarrelled with, and killed his father, not knowing who he was. On reaching Thebes he solved the Sphinx's riddle and married Jocasta
911. The principle that happiness (defined in terms of pleasure) is the sole and proper aim of human action
912. Carl Gustav Jung (1875-1961)
913. An object, usually a plant or an animal, revered by an individual or a social group
914. Soren Kierkegaard (1813-55)
915. Socrates drew forth knowledge from his pupils by pursuing a series of questions and examining the implications of the answers
916. Advaita-Vedanta
917. Bertrand Russell
918. The nature of knowledge and the process of knowing

919. Which medieval philosopher of Islam was a physician as well?
920. What is psychologism?
921. Who propounded the idea of philosopher kings?
922. What is a Freudian slip?
923. Who was the first Stoic philosopher?
924. Which ancient philosopher was called the Stagirite?
925. Who used the phrase *tabula rasa* (a blank tablet) to describe the state of human mind at birth?
926. What does *tao* mean?
927. What does Zen Buddhism hold?
928. What is *Zeitgeist?*
929. What is incontinence in the philosophical context?
930. What is the First Cause in philosophy?
931. What is *Weltanschauung?*
932. An IQ above 140 is the mark of a genius. In a modern intelligence test how many would expect to score that or above?
933. Of the three categories of persons with low IQs, morons, imbeciles, and idiots, whose intelligence is the lowest?
934. What is an agnostic?
935. What are the six systems of Hindu philosophy?
936. What is scepticism?
937. Of the low intelligence groups, morons, imbeciles, and idiots, who are capable of doing what?
938. Who is considered to be the father of modern philosophy (he was also a renowned mathematician)?
939. What are *mandala* in Hindu or Buddhist art?
940. Which ancient philosopher was known as the Angelic Doctor (*Doctor Angelicus*)?

919. Avicenna or Ibn Sina (980-1037)
920. The theory that psychology is the foundation of philosophy
921. Plato (*c.* 428-*c.* 348 B.C.)
922. Any action, such as a slip of the tongue, that may reveal an unconscious thought
923. Zeno of Citium (*c.* 334-262 B.C.)
924. Aristotle, who was born in Stagira
925. John Locke (1632-1704)
926. The Way
927. That contemplation of one's essential nature, to the exclusion of all else, is the only way of achieving pure enlightenment
928. The spirit of the time, as reflected in literature, philosophy, etc.
929. Weakness of will (knowing that it is better to do action x, but doing y intentionally)
930. God ('a First Efficient Cause, to which everyone gives the name "God" ' — St. Thomas Aquinas)
931. World outlook
932. ½%
933. Idiots
934. A person who believes that it is not possible to say definitely whether or not there is a God
935. Vedanta, Mimamsa, Samkhya, Yoga, Nyaya, and Vaisheshika
936. The philosophical attitude that certain knowledge of reality is unattainable
937. IQ 50-70, morons : can learn useful tasks and adjust under supervision
IQ 25-50, imbeciles: have to live in an institution, but can care for simple personal wants and avoid simple dangers
IQ below 25; idiots: can't do any of the above
938. Rene Descartes (1596-1650)
939. Sacred designs symbolizing the universe
940. St. Thomas Aquinas (*c.* 1225-74)

941. What is *angst* as understood in existential philosophy?
942. What is *argumentum ad baculum* in logic?
943. How is Buridan's ass associated with decision making?
944. Which ancient Indian philosopher provided the philosophical basis for the cult of *bhakti*?
945. Charvaka, Ajivika, Lokayata — what have these terms in common?
946. Who said, *cogito ergo sum*, I think, therefore I am, the argument for the basic certainty of one's existence?
947. What is cosmogony?
948. What is ESP?
949. From which ancient philosopher's name has the term dunce been derived?
950. Which Indian philosopher in the twentieth century has been a proponent of Advaita-Vedanta?

20

POTPOURRI

951. What is a potpourri proper?
952. What was the Weimar Republic?
953. What is a byte in a computer?
954. What then is a megabyte?
955. How many people must there be in a place of work to form a recognized trade union in India?
956. One of the celebrated Dadaist paintings is that of Mona Lisa adorned with a moustache and a goatee. Who was the painter?
957. How many years did it take 20,000 men to finish the Taj Mahal?

941. The dread occasioned by man's realization that his existence is open towards an unspecified future, the emptiness of which must be filled by his freely chosen action
942. The argument of the cudgel (using force to persuade)
943. The story illustrates the problem of choosing between two equally attractive alternatives. The ass, faced with two equally desirable bales of hay, starves to death because there is no reason to prefer one to the other
944. Ramanuja (12th century A.D.)
945. Alternative names of Indian materialism
946. Rene Descartes
947. A scientific or mythic account of the origin of the Universe
948. Extrasensory perception; telepathy or clairvoyance
949. John Duns Scotus (c. 1266-1388). Far from being a dunce, he was one of the most subtle of Scholastic philosophers
950. Sarvepalli Radhakrishnan (1888-1975)

20
ANSWERS

951. Originally, a pot of mixed dried flower petals kept in a room to sweeten the air; from this the other meaning of a miscellany is derived
952. The German Republic between the end of World War I and Hitler becoming the Chancellor of Germany (1919-1933)
953. A storage unit, equal to one character or eight bits
954. A storage unit equal to 1,048,576 bytes
955. 7
956. Marcel Duchamp (1887-1968)
957 22

958. Which country did Quisling betray to the Nazis?
959. What is a bug in a computer?
960. Qutb-ud-din began, but couldn't finish, the Minar named after him. Who completed it?
961. What are robots increasingly used for in heavy industries in the developed countries of the world?
962. For which language couldn't the Sahitya Akademi make any award in the first five years of its existence, 1955-59, because nothing came up to its high standards?
963. Which bacteria-killing enzyme do tears contain?
964. Apart from making films, Satyajit Ray has distinguished himself in one kind of writing. Can you name which?
965. Which country is said to have invented tourism as an industry?
966. Which is the smallest State in the world?
967. Which country, Muslim, has nevertheless declared itself as the world's first atheist State?
968. Nazi Germany called itself the Third Reich. What were the first two Reichs?
969. What is a Catch-22 situation, as described by Joseph Heller in his war novel *Catch-22*?
970. Who is the author of *Zen and the Art of Motorcycle Maintenance*?
971. For what purpose are low-flying satellites used?
972. Where will the 1994 World Cup be played?
973. How does one obtain a doctorate in Judo?
974. Which Mughal emperor issued an order that no woman should be allowed to follow the practice of suttee?
975. Which major world power never became a member of the League of Nations?
976. Which part of Britain did the Germans occupy in World War II?
977. In which country was Boris Pasternak's *Dr. Zhivago* first published?

958. Norway (1942)
959. An error in a program
960. Iltutmish
961. Welding
962. English
963. Lysozyme
964. Detective stories
965. Switzerland
966. Vatican City (0.44 sq km)
967. Albania
968. The Holy Roman Empire (962-1806) and Bismarck's Empire (1871-1918)
969. You don't have to fly any more missions if you are crazy, but if you ask to be grounded that shows you are not crazy.
970. R.M. Pirsig
971. Espionage
972. The USA
973. By attaining the highest grade, the 12th Dan
974. Aurangzeb
975. The USA
976. The Channel Islands
977. Italy

978. In which field of sport has Edson Arantes do Nascimento distinguished himself?

979. Which book contains the most detailed account of the Hitler years?

980. Who owns Macao, the 6-square-mile area in South-East China?

981. Which countries were members of the United Arab Republic?

982. George V changed the family name of the rulers of England to the House of Windsor during World War I. What was it before?

983. Which U.S. politician attained considerable notoriety by his witch hunt of Communists and Communist sympathisers in public life as well as government in the late forties and early fifties?

984. What is the function of a diode?

985. Which is the latest material used for making computer chips?

986. Which was Prophet Muhammad's favourite animal?

987. In a mosquito infested place which colour of clothes would attract the insects least?

988. Of the various sources of light, sound, and heat, whose radiation is the most harmful to human beings?

989. What did the gas plant in Bhopal which leaked methyl isocyanate manufacture?

990. Which country's flag flies oftenest on the masts of ships which do not wish to fly their own?

991. Where in modern India would Kekaya be, from which King Dasaratha's wife Kaikeyi came?

992. What is the weather criterion of calling a place a desert?

993. Which flower arrangement originally developed as offerings to the Buddha?

994. Christian Dior, Michelle Meiland, Superstar, and Peace — what do these have in common?

978. Football; he is Pele
979. William L. Shirer: *The Rise and Fall of the Third Reich*
980. Portugal
981. Egypt, Syria and Yemen
982. House of Saxe-Coburg
983. Senator Joseph Raymond McCarthy
984. It converts A.C. into D.C.
985. Gallium arsenide
986. Cat
987. White
988. Colour TV
989. Pesticides
990. Panama (called the flag of convenience)
991. Punjab, between the rivers Chenab and Jhelum
992. Less than 250 mm mean annual rainfall
993. Ikebana
994. All are tea roses of different varieties

995. Which is the toughest grass known to man?
996. Can elephants swim?
997. What is space junk?
998. Has Britain been ever without a king?
999. Which fish produces the eggs that are called caviar?
1000. Can you derive the origin of the word 'quiz'? .

21

THROWAWAYS

1a. By how much does the global temperature need to fall to bring in the ice age?
2a. What is heavy water, used as a moderator in nuclear reactors?
3a. When did Sir J.N. Tata found TISCO?
4a. Which city in Soviet Russia was renamed Stalingrad, and after deStalinization what is its new name?
5a. Which developed country in the world has no nuclear programme?
6a. Which famous composer's music was banned in Nazi Germany because he was a Jew?
7a. What is the value of a rupee in 1990 at the 1960-61 prices?
8a. Between which two places was the first railway train run in India?
9a. Which particular micro-organism has been genetically altered to eat up oil spills in water?
10a. To which country does the island Greenland belong?
11a. Is it possible for a computer to philosophize?
12a. When was the PIN code introduced in India?
13a. Where is Mount Ararat, where Noah's ark landed after the great flood?
14a. In which year was the Project Tiger launched in the country?

995. Bamboo
996. Yes, they are very good swimmers
997. Pieces of spacecraft, artificial rockets and satellites abandoned in the space
998. Yes, between 1649-60, the period of Cromwell's Protectorate
999. Sturgeon
1000. No one knows how the word was made up

21

ANSWERS

1a. 4°C
2a. Deuterium oxide
3a. 1907
4a. Tsaritsyn; Volgograd
5a. Japan
6a. Felix Mendelssohn (1809-47)
7a. 14 paise
8a. Bombay to Thane; 34 km
9a. Pseudomonas
10a. Denmark
11a. No. Abstract thought is not its cup of tea
12a. 1972
13a. Turkey
14a. 1973

15a. On which book is the enormously successful English musical *Cats* based?

16a. The plane that dropped the atomic bomb on Hiroshima was touchingly named after the pilot's mother. What was her name?

17a. Which James Bond film has a famous Indian tennis player playing a role?

18a. In which children's classic a parrot screams from time to time, 'Pieces of eight, pieces of eight'?

19a. Give the meaning of innocuous:
(a) Harmless (b) Innocent (c) Unspoilt (d) Virtuous

20a. Who said, 'An unexamined life is not worth living'?

21a. Iraq is one of the largest producers of oil in the Middle East, but it has to pipe its oil through other countries to ports. Which countries does it have to depend upon?

22a. In which field of philosophy did the French novelist Jean-Paul Sartre distinguish himself?

23a. Which is the home of litchis, or lychees (as they are spelt and pronounced in the West)?

24a. Which Indian swimmer swam them all: Palk Straits, Gibraltar Straits, the Bosphorus, the Dardanelles, the Panama Canal, and the English Channel?

25a. What does ecology literally mean?

15a. T.S. Eliot's *Old Possum's Book of Practical Cats*
16a. Enola Gay
17a. *Octopussy*; Vijay Amritraj
18a. *Treasure Island*
19a. (a)
20a. Socrates
21a. Turkey, Jordan and Saudi Arabia
22a. Existential philosophy
23a. China
24a. Mihir Sen
25a. The study of home, i.e., the environment in which one lives